Death Speaks

Death Speaks

CAROL JOAN CAMPBELL

ISBN   978-1-953150-72-1   (Paperback
ISBN   978-1-953150-73-8   (Digital)

Lettra Press books may be ordered through booksellers or by contacting: Lettra Press LLC
30 N Gould St. Suite 4753 Sheridan, WY 82801
1 307-200-3414 | info@lettrapress.com www.lettrapress.com

Death Speaks
by Carol Joan Campbell Lettra Press

"Her eyes stared up at me with a pathetic look of horror in them, and I barely heard her whisper 'Why?'"

The dire effects of untreated mental health challenges are on full display in Campbell's narrative revolving around the aftermath of a cold-blooded murder. The central character, Bill, reflects upon slaying his mother-in-law while tracing back to every part of the deed to ensure that it would appear like a robbery. Calculating and sinister, Bill's mind is on a jarring journey, a "peeling back of the curtain" to see into the mind of a psychopath.

On the one hand, the author's portrayal of Bill's mental health turmoil in medical school lends sympathy to his character. However, the meticulous manner in which he plans the murder, removing every potential roadblock that could point back to him, is downright harrowing. Conjure the image of a victim staring up into the perpetrator's eyes, asking "Why?" while the perpetrator, entirely devoid of emotion, is thinking about the crime scene as a work of photography. Perhaps what's more intriguing is his seemingly genuine fondness for Mac, his father-in-law, and his own wife, Rosie.

Leading a largely normal life at Conner's Computer Programming Company, where he is in a relatively functional relationship with his at-the-time girlfriend Rosie, Bill begins to revert into his old ways when he sees Ella constantly chastising Mac and later when Rosie is doing the same to him as she gains control of the company. More than anything else, the narrative zooms into the thought process of a killer whose absence of emotion is never more apparent than in the way he is depicted during intimate romantic moments that focus almost entirely on sensual gratification rather than a union of love. With the subsequent breakdown on the horizon, the seemingly perfect crime unraveling leaves Bill terrified in a story that descends into the darkest recesses of the mind to see if anything salvageable exists.

book review by Mihir Shah
US REVIEW OF BOOKS

CONTENTS

PART 3

Part 1

Chapter One

THE DEED WAS DONE

Ella was dead! My dear, sweet mother-in-law was really dead. I walked along the dark street acting as calmly as I could, but inside I was still churning. *I slowly went over every detail fixing it all in my mind and wondering if everything had been done right.* I was anxious to get back to my apartment - back to my familiar surroundings, but I didn't want to walk too quickly so that I would draw any attention to myself, I certainly wasn't anxious for anyone I knew to see me this evening. As often as I had thought I'd love to be over six feet tall, and exceedingly good looking, I was now glad that I just blended in with the crowd. Luckily, I was familiar with the routes from my place to Ella's condo and I had chosen a way I knew was seldom used by the majority of people. Besides, it wasn't the most pleasant evening to just be out strolling around. Yes, another one of my considerations in preparations for this evening.

I went through the scene in my head once again- sort of like a re-run of a DVD.

I'd better put that on hold and just concentrate on getting home. Wait though - what did I do with my gloves? Think Bill, think. OK, I took off the surgical scrub gown, put it in the plastic bag but I was sure that I had my gloves on the whole time until I had done what I had to do - wouldn't want to make a mistake and leave any fingerprints would I? At that thought I gave a slightly audible chuckle and noticed an inquisitive stare from an elderly lady who was passing by. How stupid of me - this was no time to act strangely. Calm down you idiot. I couldn't help but think of it- the police would find my fingerprints all over in Ella's condo, as I was there at least two or three times a week and had been for years. Yet there were certain things that I didn't want to leave any fingerprints on. That's when I remembered that I had put the surgical gloves, being very careful to turn them inside out as I took them off, in the small plastic bag I had brought with so that no blood would get on anything. I had truly worked everything out - nothing could ruin it now.

I walked along as casually as possible down the dark streets, now getting lighter as I came closer to the strip mall along the way, the one that was near the main intersection not far from her condo. Many is the time I had met Ella there, either to have dinner with her, or just to run over and pick up something for her as a favor. Now that was a MOST usual occurrence.

As I walked by Wright's Boutique, I saw a sharp looking azure blue dress on the gorgeous, perfect blonde mannequin standing in the window - smiling brilliantly with bright pink lips and deep blue eyes. Perhaps a little too perfect looking - well what would you expect, after all, she's not human. I couldn't help but think how beautiful my Lola would look in that dress. It even brought back a memory of my Dad, Mitchell Anderson, a man I adored and admired. He was always such a perfect gentleman, soft spoken and so loving. He and my Mom, Laura were truly in love - even as the years passed by. She was an attractive woman - perhaps not gorgeous, but in my Dad's eyes she was. Mom's favorite color was blue, and she always looked so pretty when wearing it. Even more so as she got older and her hair turned to a silvery gray. Her eyes were always bright blue, and sparkled when she laughed, and she did smile and laugh a lot. Dad would look at her when they were dressed up to go out with friends, many times wearing blue, which was her favorite color. He would sing an old song that I guess was popular when he was young. *Let's see - how did it go again? Oh yeah, "In your sweet little Alice blue gown, when I first took you out on the town".* Hmmm - not sure if those were the exact words, but he had a strong, pleasant voice, and sometimes I thought she got a little teary eyed when he'd sing a few lines to her and then give her a little kiss on the cheek.

Oh, we had a good life growing up, Mom, Dad, my sister Susie, my little brother Gary, big brother Jim and myself. OK, back to reality - time to reminisce when you get home.

One more glance at that dress though - now, I thought *I'll really be able to dress Lola in fantastic outfits.* My darling Lola was one of those gals who, whenever you asked her out anywhere, always said that she didn't have anything to wear. When I was at her place and got glances in her closet, she certainly seemed to have plenty of clothes of every variety and in every color - not to mention all of the shoes scattered on the floor. Well, at any rate, I'd take care of her now - I'd get her all of the clothes that she wanted. I used to tease her by singing that old song "Whatever Lola wants, Lola gets". Just realized I guess I do have some of my Dad's traits - here I was doing the same thing - falling back on old songs to express some of my feelings. Right then I decided to go back tomorrow morning and buy that dress for her.

I started walking but stopped at a window that was tinted green and looked at the slight reflection that was allowed by the street lights and neon advertising signs along the street. I couldn't see too much, but I could make out a man, perhaps 6 feet, 3 inches tall - he was wearing a police uniform. I suddenly felt almost queasy, but he walked quietly on by. I resumed the study of my own reflection. No, I decided, no one would think that this5 foot 11 man with blond, slightly graying hair and blue eyes would have done anything wrong. No, I assured myself, I was quite safe, and again I was most thankful that I was just an ordinary looking man. At this thought I couldn't help but smile, for I remembered all of the times that I had wished that I might look outstandingly special, so that when I walked down the street people would look around at me and murmur to their friends how " nice looking" I was. I suppose that way of thinking was tucked away in my mind from high school days - you know how during those wonderful, but terrible teen years when I suppose every guy wants to be a good looking football hero - elected as Homecoming King, walking out on the dance floor escorting the most beautiful, witty, remarkable female in the class who of course was elected as Homecoming Queen. Those were just old dreams, but never quite forgotten. Well, better hurry on, get off the streets and get home. There will be plenty of time to think about everything then. It is strange, however that I seemed to be falling back into thinking of old days - trying to stay on a positive note, but sometimes more and more lately those terrible and frightful months when I'd had the break down keep creeping in. *No, can't afford to think of that now.*

Chapter 2

TIME TO SLOW DOWN
AND THINK

When I got home, I finally felt completely safe again and knew I only had a few more details to take care of before I forgot and made any mistakes. I took off my overcoat and hung it up. Then I went out to the kitchen and got some plastic disposable gloves from the bottom drawer, put them on and then went back to the closet. I had taken off the surgical gown very carefully and placed it in a larger plastic bag which I had sitting open, ready to fill after everything was done. That's when I took my gloves off, put them in with the gown and stuffed it all in the large inside pocket of my coat. That's why I chose that coat to wear - it was one that I bought when we were going on a trip. I had never seen one with such a large inside pocket and figured it would be handy to stash things in while we were traveling.

Good thinking, Bill - now you were already prepared to work out the final details to do the deed and protect myself. There, let's go back to another old refrain - from an old mystery show - can't remember which one for sure. think it was something about names being changed to protect the innocent. Stop it Bill, you're fading back into old memories far too often lately.

OK. Everything was almost taken care of. I pulled the plastic bag out and brought it over to the fireplace. I already had the makings for the fire ready to go – yes, I had every detail worked out. I lit the fire - I had plenty of paper and kindling, so it started easily, and a couple of the precious birch logs that I usually saved for special events caught hold. Well, this was certainly a special event. I waited a while until it was burning quite nicely, and then threw in the plastic bag, which melted quickly, and any small remnants of gown and gloves quickly disappeared. I then went into the bedroom, got undressed and took a long hot shower, soaping down generously, but never even noticed any blood anywhere. For the first time I felt sort of strange - almost queasy, and it scared me. I'd had that feeling before during my breakdown. *Stop it* - maybe it's just that I stood under the shower for so long, and it was a hot one - evidenced by the fact that the whole bathroom seemed enveloped in dense steam even though I had the exhaust fan going. I walked over to the sink and used my towel to wipe off a circle so I could look at myself. The reflection was sort of weird, kind of spooky with steam swirling around it - *again I thought of all of those images that floated around in my head when I was in the hospital in those teen years.*

Now I was angry at myself, I had locked all of those thoughts away for so long - why were they nagging at me now? I turned away, finished wiping myself off and decided that I probably just needed a good stiff drink and at least some cheese and crackers or a hunk of meat or something. *Yah, that's what's the matter, I'm just hungry.*

I put on my pajamas and robe, went out into the kitchen and got some cheese, crackers and ham that was left from dinner last night and put it all on a plate. Then I went over to the cupboard where I kept my bar supplies - got out one of the biggest glasses that I could find and mixed myself an extremely large drink - a victory drink, if you will. I walked back into the living room, settled in to my favorite chair - the luxurious big recliner, made sure the TV remote was readily available and finally took a good long drink and started to just relax. I was going to watch TV, but I never even turned it on. As I took a few more sips of my drink and ate the food, I found my thoughts drifting back to the death scene in Ella's condo. I smiled at that recollection and started reconstructing the crime.

Chapter 3

THE PLAN EVOLVED

Ella came home from work at 6:15 each night. I had discovered from her financial records that she didn't have to work, but she had bought a small consignment shop in the mall not far from her place. She only had it open from 12:30 to 5:30. I had carefully checked out the time element. I had watched her from across the street six nights - hidden in a shadowy area of course so that no one would notice me. There had been times when I had actually been a part of her procedure, but I wanted to make sure that it was the same whether I was there or not. She had occasionally asked me over for dinner, suggesting that I stop at the shop and walk home with her, explaining that she would get the groceries we needed before she opened up the shop. She had a little refrigerator in the back of the shop, so she'd just put everything in there. Then, if I stopped and met her, I could help by carrying the groceries home for her and then she would make dinner for the two of us. She was, I must admit, a pretty good cook. At any rate, as I stood outside and watched, she seemed to follow the exact routine each night. She pressed in the security code, and as she closed the door, she snapped on the light switch. Next, she would go out to the kitchen, turn on the little TV and start to make dinner. I had actually thought at first of rigging up a bomb somehow to either the light or the TV, but that was so complicated - of course the police would know then that it was a murder - if it succeeded. That was the other thing, it might not be fatal and guess who'd be stuck with taking care of her - good old

Bill. Besides, I wanted her to die by my hand, by my cleverness – oh yes, I wanted everything to be carried out by me.

The next part of the plan had possibly been that of hiding, grabbing her from behind and strangling her, but then I got to thinking that if she started to struggle, I might not be strong enough to succeed in killing her. I wasn't exactly the most athletic person who enjoyed enhancing muscles by lifting weights or anything, and Ella was not much shorter than me, and pretty strong herself. Then I came up with the final plan - even consulted medical books to find critical areas, and now I had the perfect plan.

I couldn't help but think back about my time in medical school. *Yes, I had decided that I really wanted to be a doctor - help people, save lives, be somebody's hero every day. I was accepted and had enrolled at the State University. I was one excited student. Mom and Dad were so proud of me - I had higher goals set for myself than my sister and brothers had. Somehow, I had always felt not quite so good about myself as my older brother Jim. He was tall, good looking and popular with everyone. He always seemed to have loads of friends coming over to see him, everyone calling him all of the time. I couldn't seem to compete with him - well, maybe compete wasn't the right word, he certainly never made me feel inferior, and we had lots of good times together - maybe I just admired him too much.*

He was only two years older than me, so even when he tried to include me in some of his fun, I many times just felt like a tag-along. He never did go on to further his education. He and a friend took off for California for a couple of years after he graduated from High School, and while there, he joined the Navy and was out and about for four years. After he got back home, he became a salesman, first selling cars, which my Dad had done for most of his life, and then went into the insurance field, and is indeed most successful. He's married and has a couple of kids, so all turned out good.

At any rate, I still had my medical books, and found myself looking at them occasionally, but when I made the decision about Ella, I actually studied them again - to find the best information as to how to carry this whole thing off. From those days I also had a couple of surgical gowns and latex gloves packed away, and then the rest of the plan just sort of evolved.

It was while Jim was in the Navy that I was finally heading into medical school. I really took to it at first, and even made some friends along the way. Of course, there wasn't much spare time to socialize a lot - just stuck to the books, and never got enough sleep. I know that Mom and Dad saw things weren't right, and they made me come home on weekends so that I could get some good food, and just rest up, but things were getting tough. I started getting behind in everything - I was having trouble making passing grades, and my self- doubts started mounting up. I kept pushing myself -everything became a struggle and the worse it got the worse I felt. I knew that Mom and Dad were getting really worried now. They even suggested that I drop out for a quarter and maybe go on a little vacation with them, but to me, that would be giving up, and I told them I was fine. Mom made me go to the doctor - figuring that perhaps he could convince me that it would be better to step back for a while. He however said I was just fine, and that college was good for me. Well, he may have been influenced by knowing that I was in medical school, and he probably had gone through just as many rough months himself when he was there

I remember, I just couldn't sleep - I kept pushing - the voices in my head started, I couldn't even stand to watch TV. It was like I was being controlled by a stranger - that's when I had the complete terrible breakdown. I'll never forget that - I was at home luckily, I guess. I was floating further and further away from reality and getting angrier and angrier with people who kept asking me if everything was OK and if they could do anything to help me. The worst offender of course was Mom - my darling Mom. She wanted so desperately to help me - of course I really knew that, but I was feeling more and more angry - wishing that she would just leave me alone. She was always trying to be so calm, to talk to me - to see what she could do and suggest that I find some help. All the time I kept building up resentments towards it I felt like I was an animal and she was armed with a prodding iron - trying to get me back in control. I don't know how I could have done it, but one day I just couldn't stand it anymore, and when she asked me if a cup of coffee or cocoa might help, I lost it. I attacked her!! I don't know how I could have done it, but she just seemed at that moment to be the cause of all of the problems. I wrestled her down to the ground and put my hands around her neck. She started crying and said "No Bill, don't do it, don't do it". I got up, went over to the fireplace and picked up the poker. When she saw that she ran out the back door. Soon the police were there, then the ambulance, and I ended up in the hospital. OK Bill - stop it.

I thought I had pushed all of that out of my mind –I don't want to dredge it up now. This is the time when I'm going to have to be in control of myself and remember everything. I figured I'd better mix another drink. I didn't want to drink too much and make my thoughts fuzzy, but also thought it would calm me down a bit. I went over to the bar area and mixed another one - not too strong, but generous.

Chapter 4

WHEN ROSIE CAME ALONG.

When I got calmed down a bit, I thought back on my days with Rosie so now I'll tell you more. There were lots of good days. After I finally recovered from the break down, I got a good job. I started as a teller in the local bank, and from there on got into accounting, and finally after a couple of business courses, did work into the accounting department of Conner's Computer Programming Company. - Owned by Mac and Ella Conner, and Rosie, their daughter worked there.

Rosie pretty much knew the business from every aspect. In fact, when anyone was out sick for a day, Rosie could usually take over. Back in Mom and Dad's day, they would have called her 'Our Gal Friday', but now-a-days women sort of seem to resent that moniker - I always thought it was really a compliment. I liked Mac, he was one of these Type A people, probably sort of a workaholic, but usually very pleasant. His wife Ella I guess had worked in the company for many years, but then stepped down to take care of Rosie. She was an only child, so I guess they figured that raising her was the most important work at the moment. Granted, Rosie was probably a hand full during her teen years, for she was bright all right, and fairly attractive - dark hair, beautiful completion and extremely dark blue eyes - well I suppose some would say she was more than just attractive, and I imagine when I first got to know her, I thought so too.

With no male heirs to carry on the business, Mac started priming

Rosie as a possible next CEO of Conner's, and she took it very seriously, and did a good job of it. Mac hired lots of experts in the field, and it was sort of a stipulation that they had to work with Rosie for a while - sort of training her in. I suppose some said it was a cheap way of getting her education and Dad could still keep her on the pay roll and pay her while she was learning off of others knowledge. Well, more power to him - that's why he owned the company instead of being just an employee.

At any rate, Rosie learned well. When she came into my area, I worked really close to her, and I do mean close - you know, working on the books, sitting close together by the computer, searching old files, etc. I somehow got to like the feeling of having her near me. She always wore a light perfume, but with sort of a musky smell that almost made me feel a little light headed. Occasionally her long dark hair would brush against me. At times when she leaned over my shoulder, her sumptuous breast would touch me, and I began to have wild dreams about what it would be like to have her in my arms, gently caress her and unbutton her blouse and be able to touch her bare breasts. In my mind I could feel the smoothness of that soft, skin and feel her firm nipples get even harder when I touched them - and she would make wonderful, little gasping sounds, and want to satisfy any basic needs that I might have. Guess it became inevitable that I asked her out - even though I was afraid it might not be the right thing to do. There was only one way to know for sure. I asked her out on a date, and she accepted. I didn't tell anyone at work about our date, as I wasn't sure how they would take it, and of course I didn't know what the evening might bring - if we'd hit it off at all, or just what. Better just to wait and see how things went - figured they would all find out about it soon enough if indeed it did develop.

I always loved to think back on our first date. We started out with a typical evening - dinner at a good restaurant, but not the fanciest one in town. I made a good living but was always rather conservative. Mom and Dad always lived comfortably, but they had taught all of us not to go overboard and get into financial trouble. Perhaps that's why I decided to get into accounting, so that I could learn to budget and save along the way - the sensible thing to do. At any rate, we went to a movie after - a rather light hearted one - not exactly what I would have picked, but of course I let her do the choosing. I do know that I found it wonderful just to be sitting next to her and feel her closeness. Towards the end of the movie, I did put my arm around her, and she didn't back away - just leaned closer. I can't tell you much about the movie, but I do remember how I felt, and I made the decision that I really would like to see more of her - and I meant that literally too. Oh, we had some wonderful times, and we were always walking hand in hand, and her good night kisses were getting more passionate all of the time. I always tried to be a gentleman, but it was getting harder and harder to restrain myself, and each time that I was with her, I fell more in love with her and found I wanted to be with her longer than just occasionally.

Eventually I began to be known as Rosie's boyfriend - sure I took some razing from some of the other guys at work, but then I didn't care. By now I was really feeling what I knew was love for her. I had had a few relationships, but nothing that I really wanted to turn into anything too serious. Those gals were just a diversion - granted I wined and dined a few long enough to have my sexual desires satisfied, and perhaps that's all I was really interested in. It just seemed that after a bit I would get tired of them and gradually drop off. Never broke my heart, and seemingly never broke theirs either.

After not too long, I was able to fulfill some of my sexual dreams about Rosie. I'll never forget the first time. She was over at my apartment, it was a winter evening, so I had started a fire in the fireplace. I mixed a drink for both of us, and we sat close together, enjoying the fire. I had a really nice CD playing, sort of Semi Classical, but soft and romantic, it was wonderful. She got up and lit a couple of candles that I had on the side table, turned out the lights and came back and cuddled up with me. I took that as possibly an invitation. I put my arm around her, gave her some soft kisses, and then pressed my hand against her breast. She sighed but didn't move away. I then progressed with my long-ago dream, my hand went inside of her blouse, and still she didn't move away. I took off my shirt. Now I took both hands, and undressed her - being very gentle, and moving my hands over each portion of her body as it lay exposed. Her body was gorgeous - I pressed both of my hands over those beautiful breasts, and they felt soft and wonderful. My penis responded by swelling so that I had to pull my pants down and give it freedom.

By now I was trying to slow myself down – I'd had sex before, but never with anyone that I had such special feelings for. I knew then that this may be the REAL time. I picked her up and carried her into the bedroom. That slowed me down for a moment, but the arousal started again as we got into bed. We wrestled passionately for a bit, feeling skin to skin and body to body - it was complete ecstasy. I now was touching her and kissing her all over and every time she pressed her whole self against my bare body, it felt fantastic, but I couldn't stray far from those beautiful breasts. We thrashed back and forth, and the frenzy grew with each touch. Finally, I mounted above her, and she arched her body in the most wonderful way, put her arms tightly around me and made more delicious sounds. Then I found I couldn't hold out any longer. I pushed my swollen penis into her waiting cavity, trying to keep it as gentle and slow as possible. As I did, she started arching higher and making moaning sounds like I had never heard before. She gave a final arch, and I came at the same moment with a muffled cry of joy myself. Oh, it was good. We were truly one. I'd never felt so like a real man before, and fell back into bed next to her, put my arms around her and contentment surrounded both of us. Yes, I was sure now, this was the woman I really wanted to marry.

Chapter 5

ENTERING ROSIE'S FAMILY

Over the next year, I sort of edged right into the Conner's family. I have to admit that it was fun to be in the company of the "elite" society - one can't help but be caught up in the whirl of fancy dinner parties, plays, being welcomed and immediately seated at the best restaurants in town. I hadn't exactly grown up in such surroundings.

Mom and Dad hadn't ever traveled in such circles. My sister Susie on the other hand had married quite well and she had adapted very nicely to those things. To my folk's amazement. she fell into a life style that she adored - a nice enough guy who owned a big ranch, among other ventures. Oh, how she loved horses - any animal you could imagine, as a matter of fact. She was good with all of them. Susie was a most attractive gal, sort of a strawberry blonde, slim, but very strong. She loved the outdoors, and riding her horse was her favorite thing to do. She hadn't finished college, just there long enough to meet Ron, and fell like a ton of bricks, and obviously the feeling was shared by him. True, the marriage didn't last long - only 3 years. I guess she fell more for the animals than she did for Ron, and he finally had had enough. He started a lot of flings which Susie soon found out about. I think she found it pretty loathsome, but figured that if that's what he wanted, so be it, she'd just live it up and do as she pleased. She moved into one of the other bedrooms - with an inside lock on the door. Ron finally found her to be just too much trouble - he wanted to slide back into his old freedom. He finally opted to ask for a divorce. She didn't seem to mind - provided she ended up with the ranch and horses and enough income to be able to stay there for as long as she may want. She always seemed very happy and was fun to be with. She had lots of friends to keep busy doing things with, so I guess it worked out for the best for both of them. Mom died the year after Susie got married, so she didn't have to go through the pain of seeing it not work out. Dad lived for a couple more years - eventually moving in with Susie. She had plenty of room, and he always enjoyed being out there where he could help her when he was still able to, and for Jim, Gary and myself, it worked out well too, as she took good care of him when his health started turning bad. Susie loved him dearly and pampered him, but was happy for his company, which the rest of us felt good about. In fact, we all felt pretty indebted to her, but she did it with a loving heart, and never made us feel that we weren't doing enough. We all took turns going out there on a regular basis, occasionally all of us at the same time, and it was sort of like a family reunion. We had all gotten along so well - and had good times together. Dad still loved to sing some of the old songs, and if we knew them, we joined in, if not, we just sat back and listened and encouraged him to continue.

I did include Rosie at some of these get together, but I got the feeling that she wasn't quite so happy about them as the rest of the family. Gary was married now, and his wife always seemed to have a good time as did Jim's family, but Rosie always seemed a little more quiet than usual. In fact, Gary had talked to me about her - asking me if I was sure that I really wanted to build a relationship with her, and of course at that time, that's exactly what I wanted. She always knew how to make me feel wonderful, and I was sure no one else could satisfy me as she did. Gary always seemed to be the one who could think everything out and look things over carefully and not jump into anything too quickly. I admired that in him and respected his opinion, but I had feelings for Rosie that I felt would never go away.

In the meantime, I did feel more and more comfortable being over with the Conner's. I could see though that Ella was a tough cookie to live with. Mac didn't seem to pay too much attention, but she was always harping at him for something - either the way he was dressed, the way he ate, the way he acted. No one else seemed to notice, so I convinced myself that it was just the way they were, and who was I to meddle in any affairs? Besides, by now I was truly in love with beautiful Rosie. We had many fun times together, and our sexual lives were unbelievable There were times when I could hardly wait for evenings out with other people to be over so that I could get back to the apartment and travel into another surprising and wonderful sexual orgy. It was hard to get up and take her home, but after a couple of months, she suggested how nice it would be if she could just crawl over in my bed and stay overnight. That arrangement fell right into my way of thinking. She even brought a few outfits and put them in the closet so that if it was a work day, she could just get ready for work and we'd drive in together. I wasn't always quite ready to announce our relationship status quite so readily to everyone at work, so I insisted that I drop her off around the corner where she could get on an enclosed walkway and I would continue and park in the private underground parking area for the Conner people. I think it sort of ticked her off, but back then, she'd still do a few things just because I wanted it that way. All I know is that if she would have said she wasn't going to stay overnight with me if I didn't inform everyone about our relationship, I probably would have groveled at her feet and done exactly as she wanted me to. She was my goddess - my passionate lover, and I was enjoying the best sex life that I could ever have dreamt about. I never really thought about how she had learned all the things that she would do to arouse me and satisfy me, I only knew that she was the most exciting and sexiest woman that I had ever met, and when I asked her to marry me, she accepted. Back then I was floating on cloud nine.

Chapter 6

WEDDING AHEAD

We had only been engaged for 3 months when Rosie decided that we should have a Christmas wedding, and I went along for the ride. I didn't have to do much, after all, efficient Rosie and Ella would take care of everything.

It was in August when they started planning the affair. Once they found a date in late December when the church was available it became a reality. I never knew they could find so many things to get so nit-picky about, so many of them that they wanted me to be involved in. I didn't really care if the attendants wore red, green, black or whatever. I'd just smile and nod my head, and that seemed to take care of most of the arrangements. All I could think about at that time was the fact that Rosie would be with me every day and every night, and I could cuddle and touch her and touch every part of her whenever I wanted to. What was more important than that? I idolized her.

Jim and Gary were to be my attendants, and Rosie did ask Susie to be one of her attendants also. Susie wasn't exactly thrilled with Rosie, and had told me so, but I was flying high, and she wasn't about to spoil things for me, so she consented to be in the wedding also. They did eventually wear red, after all it was a Christmas wedding, and the guys were to wear plain old black tuxes - of course we had to wear red cummerbunds and red bow ties to make everything match.

I had been thinking back on so many things, I had to go over to the desk and dig a bit and find that wedding picture – yes, we were a very good-looking couple. Sort of a contrast with my blonde, light blue eyes and her dark brunette, almost black hair and those deep blue eyes. *If only Mom and Dad could have been there also. Dad had died the middle of November, but at least he knew that I had a good job, now probably guaranteed until retirement, and was headed in the direction of a normal married life - at least that's what he thought at that time. It did bring him peace.*

Being as I was up, I added some more wood to the fire and went out in the kitchen to have a few munchies - yep, some chips and dip would taste pretty good and may as well freshen up my drink at the same time. Then it was back to the recliner - turned on the TV for a while, but couldn't really concentrate on watching anything, just turned on some background music instead. The snack really tasted good, even better washed down with the drink. I knew of course that I probably wouldn't be able to sleep, but perhaps I'd try anyhow. I wasn't quite ready to crawl in bed though, so I just leaned back a little in the recliner. I finally managed to doze for about an hour.

When I woke, things seemed hazy for a few minutes - probably a result of the drinks, but still a pleasant feeling - even more pleasant as I just closed my eyes and that dredged up more memories. I still had the wedding picture out and pleasantly fell back into that memory of our wedding. *It was quite the wedding - indeed the social event of the year. We did end up getting married 2 days after Christmas, so we celebrated Christmas with all of Rosie and my family joined together at the Conner's place. It was a gorgeous, huge home, so room enough for everyone. They had hired people to prepare a home cooked dinner with all the fixings, and I know that everyone enjoyed themselves. It took our minds off the wedding for a change - I was getting to the point I didn't want to hear anything more about it. I had done everything that I had to — got measured for the tux, made sure that my brothers had also. I knew that Susie had her dress and wasn't complaining about that anyhow. I had the gifts for the guys, and a special gift for Rosie — some beautiful diamond and ruby earrings. The red to remember our Christmas wedding — of course Susie had suggested that, but I thought it would impress Rosie. After we had become engaged, I had gotten a most substantial raise in salary, so I felt I could splurge a little more than I normally would have dreamed of. I was tired of going over and over every little detail, but I knew it was important for both Rosie and Ella to have everything come up as perfection. I went along with everything, but now I just wanted it to be over. I somehow knew it would be perfect, and I'd just sit back and enjoy it, and that I did. There were probably about 450 people who attended, comfortably filling the church. It was an older one, very ornate and had beautiful stained-glass windows. There was a large one behind the altar with a beautiful picture of Jesus and the disciples. It was lighted from the outside, so all of the magnificent colors showed up vividly. The decorations that most churches have at Christmas were still in place, Christmas trees with white mini lights on them, red and white poinsettias around the altar and the pulpit, and Rosie had selected beautiful big bouquets of red and white roses on the altar.*

As I finally stood by the altar with my brothers at my side, the Wedding processional began, I watched the bridesmaids come down the aisle, noting to myself that Susie was by far the most beautiful one. I was, however, almost unprepared when they finally raised the decibel of the music and Rosie started down the aisle, with Mac walking proudly at her side. I had a hard time holding back tears, as she was such a vision to see. The beautiful white gown ornately decorated in lace, pearls and sequins made Rosie look like part of an ornate fairy tale picture. The filmy white veil almost formed a halo around her beautiful dark hair. She was gorgeous, and soon she would be mine to hold forever. As she neared the altar, there was the formal "Who gives this bride stuff, with the reply "Her mother and I do" and Mac placed her hand in mine and we walked up two steps to join the minister, and the actual wedding began.

I was very impressed with one detail that had been taken care of that I didn't even know about and hadn't thought about. Rosie had arranged for a brass vase sitting on a plant holder with 2 beautiful white roses in it, and it was announced that they were in memory of my Mom and Dad. She even had one of the soloists sing a song that my Mom and Dad had played at their wedding - "O Perfect Love". All of us as kids had sort of celebrated each of their Anniversaries by looking through their wedding book which Mom took from the shelf and had out so they could look through it and tell us stories about when the pictures were taken. They even had an audio tape of the wedding. I'm sure in some teenage years it seemed like a drudge to have to be involved in the looking and listening, but it was one of those things that we knew we had to do. There was one piece that Dad used to sing and told us how much it meant to Mom and him. "Oh Perfect Love" I had told Rosie about the yearly ritual, and she had obviously remembered. That made me feel kind of emotional, and I had to blink my eyes a bit when I heard it. Another surprise that Rosie had planned for me. Yes, it was all most impressive - even to my usually 'not noticing many details' eyes, it looked great.

We'd had most of our formal wedding pictures taken before the wedding began, so after the ceremony was over, we walked directly outside, not having a formal reception line at the church. Jim quickly gave me my overcoat, and Joan, the maid of honor was there to hand Rosie her beautiful white fur jacket so we wouldn't get cold while we walked down the many steps and got into the waiting long, white limo. Yes, every detail had indeed been taken care of and everything had been perfect.

Next was the reception, and what fun that was. We all went to the fanciest restaurant

in town - The Silverstone Lodge. We had a beautiful huge room that was all decorated up for Christmas of course, so it was even more festive looking than usual. Everyone was served champagne when they entered the room, Rosie and Ella had even made Place Cards for everyone designating what table they should sit at. Careful thought had gone into this so that everyone would know some of the people who would be seated with them. The tables were decorated beautifully with bouquets of red and white roses with evergreen branches mixed in and a glass hurricane enclosing a candle flickering beautifully in the center of each one. The tables were set with beautiful dishes and crystal goblets and white linen cloths and red napkins. We had a fantastic meal, a great salad, Prime Rib, twice baked potatoes, a mixture of vegetables, all of this accompanied with free- flowing wine for everyone. They even had a small group of musicians playing background music while we ate. *I can almost hear them now.*

As is tradition we were seated at the head table, along with the wedding party, so I had the best of worlds that anyone could have - Rosie next to me, and my brothers and my sister on the other side of me. The meal was punctuated with lots of clinking glasses - each clink meaning a mandatory kiss for Rosie and myself. That was no problem and added to the feeling of happiness and fun. Finally, there was ice cream and wedding cake for dessert.   I had never seen a wedding cake like we had before - it consisted of layers that rose like a winding staircase, all covered with red and white roses made of the tastiest frosting I had ever had. We had talked about when we cut the cake and had pictures taken, she didn't want to spoil the beauty of the moment by stuffing cake into each other's faces as we'd seen done at some other weddings. I fully agreed with her and I was content just to have one significant bite by each of us.

It seemed again like a scene out of a fairy tale, and I was the Prince and Rosie was the Princess. A few more musicians joined the group that had been playing during dinner, then the dance began. When Rosie and I were out on the dance floor alone for the first dance of the evening, it was magical. Enjoying the music and our bodies swaying together was perfect. Oh, that feeling of holding her close, feeling her body pressed close to mine and giving her kisses whenever I wanted to. It was heaven. There, another old song of Dad's - "I'm In Heaven"   thinking of some more lines, they all seemed to fit my mood at that time.

Everyone seemed to be having a good time. Being as we hadn't had a formal reception line, all through the evening we circled the room trying to spend a few minutes with all the guests. That was sort of a drudge, but one of those things that all couples should do. I was practically seeing constant spots before my eyes from all the flashes with everyone taking pictures of us. I knew my family were all having a good time. After the dinner was over, they had all joined together at one of the round tables. Jim, his wife Mary, Gary and his wife Sally and Susie completing the picture. Somehow, I couldn't help but think how much Mon and Dad would have enjoyed it, but I had to feel that they were probably watching it all and smiling down at us.

Finally, it was time for us to leave and take our waiting limo to the fanciest hotel in town where we entered the wedding suite. It was beautiful – all decorated in white and gold and a big bathroom, complete with a Jacuzzi tub. The bedroom had a fireplace with a gas flame already burning and making the room feel warm and cozy when we arrived.

I remember every detail. I had a few moments when I thought I might suggest that we sit in the hot tub and enjoy looking at one another and caressing one another for a while, but all I could think about was getting in bed with her – knowing that even though we'd had wonderful sexual adventures, this would indeed be complete, we were now husband and wife.

She took off her wedding gown, but then went into the bathroom and closed the door. While she was in there, I took off my tux and crawled into bed, waiting to see what the next act would be. She finally stepped out, and what a vision she was. She had on a gorgeous pale pink, very sheer night gown with small satin roses covering the straps and top of it.   Her hair which had been piled beautifully in curls all over her head was now hanging down over her shoulders. If any artist ever wanted a gorgeous model, Rosie was it, and she was mine. She came to me and let me look at her, feel her, undress her and pull her into bed with me. What man could ever want more from a woman - I knew I had more right now that I ever could have imagined, and I didn't think that my life ahead could ever hold anything more wonderful than what I was experiencing right now. We had sex three times that night - just resting and cuddling in between, and finally, at this point exhausted, I fell asleep, with my fantastic wife encircled in my arms.

Chapter 7

A PERFECT HONEYMOON

As a wedding gift, the Conner's had informed us that they would take care of the honeymoon. They had a condo in Grand Cayman, so that would be our destination. We had to be at the airport early the next morning. The Conner's had made all the arrangements, so there wasn't anything much that I had to do other than get up and get going in the morning. I would have loved to stay in bed and repeat last night's performance, but there would be time in the two weeks ahead, I imagined.

We got to the airport by 8:00 - had a bite to eat while we were waiting to board the plane. It was only a four- hour flight to Grand Cayman, but the Conner's had even gotten first class seating for us. *I had never really done much traveling before. Mom and Dad took us on camping trips mostly when we were small, and we always had a fantastic time, but I think at times it was harder on Mom rather than just enjoyment. As she sometimes would comment, but always saying it kiddingly (at least we thought so at the time), that camping was a lot of inconvenient housekeeping, and I suppose it was.*

A few times we went on driving trips with them and stayed in the cabins at some resorts along the way. That was a step in the right direction, and Mom I think enjoyed that much more. We at least had hot water, indoor plumbing - no trips to an outdoor biffy, and she could take a warm shower in the morning and not have to depend upon a dip into a cool lake to wash herself off. Yes, to my family, that was luxury, but we had some of the greatest memories that were always caught on camera and put into albums. Mom was good about keeping a journal every day when we traveled, and then would include all her notes along with the appropriate pictures and after it was completed, we'd all take turns flipping the pages and talking about the great time that we had had. Yes, I'd had a wonderful life growing up. Don't know why it had to go so haywire and end up with me flipping out as I had. Enough of that, Bill. I just wanted to keep the good memories and think about all the special memories to come in the lifetime of Bill and Rosie.

The flight was smooth as could be - they say it's usually smoother flying during the winter than it is in the summer, because of less turbulence, but I had only flown a half dozen times before and had never had enough bumpiness to trouble me, so I was no authority on that. Shortly after takeoff, the flight attendant had a surprise for us - they came back with a bottle of champagne and a couple of glasses. Mac and Ella had thought of everything - they even had some snacks for us, it was perfect. Before we had time to barely even finish it off, we were landing in Cayman.

When we got off the plane, I was amazed. I'd never been on a tropical island, leaving in the cold of winter with snow on the ground and suddenly 4 hours later getting off and feeling warm breezes and bright sun was magnificent. The grass was green, palm trees swaying in the breezes and flowers in bloom. What a welcome respite from winter storms. After we got through customs, it was time to head to Plantation Village on Seven Mile Beach, where Mac and Ella's condo was. While Rosie waited with the luggage, I walked across the road as Mac had instructed me to and saw Andy's Rent - A - Car. He had made all the arrangements for us to pick up a rental for our use wherever we wanted to go for the next two weeks. I drove back in our chariot, a nice white two door Toyota. Driving of course would be quite an adventure, as the Cayman's are in the British West Indies, and they drive on the left side of the street. I really had to keep my wits about me, and I wasn't sure if I really wanted to drive much at all. Oh well, it's only a small island, and I'd probably catch on to it if I took it slow. I picked up Rosie and the luggage, and then we headed off for the Condo. Rosie had been there many times before, so she knew the way, which was most helpful. She could see that I was rather nervous trying to figure out which lane I should be in when I was making a turn. If that wasn't bad enough, they had roundabouts which I had not experienced before, but with Rosie gently giving me instructions, we finally made it to our home at "Plantation", sitting right on the ocean and looking at seven miles of beautiful white sand. The color of the ocean was as aqua as I could ever imagine. I of course had only seen scenes like this in magazines and on TV, but here we were.

It was only about 4:00 by the time we were checked in, so still beautiful out and rather than unpack, we just changed into our bathing suits and headed out for the beach. We had our choice - either the ocean or the pool. I headed for the ocean - this would be my first venture. Wow, it was wonderful. The temp was good - felt brisk enough to be refreshing, but once you were in it for a bit it was just great. The feel of the waves carrying our bodies was quite a sensation, and I enjoyed every minute of it. After a bit we went back and sat on the chaise lounges on the beach and enjoyed having the sun warm us up and just relaxed. We knew we'd better not get a sun burn - everyone had warned us about that, but by now the sun wasn't quite so hot, so we ordered a drink to be served right on the beach, laid back and soaked in both the sun and the booze. I looked at Rosie seated close to me – once in a while she would reach over and touch me, and each touch got me slightly aroused. *What was Dad's old song? oh yes "Lovely to Look At - Delightful to Hold" Yep, that just sort of said it all. He was always going back to favorite songs - many times they just said things better apparently than he supposed he could have said them himself.*

Finally, we headed back to our condo. We took a shower - together - and lathering Rosie up and having her lather me up was wonderfully fun. Pressing our slippery bodies together and smelling the clean smell of the soap was almost as intoxicating as downing a strong Manhattan. My manhood arose to the occasion, and we were off on another adventure. The steam in the shower rose around us - as if I wasn't feeling steamed up enough - could anything be better than this? Married life was fantastic.

The entire two weeks we were there was an adventure - we did do some sight- seeing - as the saying in Cayman is, we went to Hell and back, learned a bit about the history of the island - back from the Pirate days, etc. Went to the Turtle Farm of course - Cayman is famous for that, and it was quite impressive. Then there was the day when we went to Sting Ray city - a boat ride on the Ocean to a fabulous place where the water is quite shallow - not far from the reef, but a special spot where the boats anchor and we got out with our snorkel equipment and walked around and actually swam with the Sting Rays and helped to feed them. They look like such ugly creatures, but when you are with them and feel their soft bodies float over you, you realize how gentle they are and see them suddenly as beautiful. *I stored all these adventures in my head.*

We ate at so many of the Restaurants that I could hardly keep track of them. Rosie of course knew the best ones, and that's where we went. For lunch one day I got most venturesome and ordered a Turtle Burger - not bad at all. We had Conch Fritters for appetizers many times, and I developed quite a liking for them. The catch of the day was always wonderful - never had had such a variety of fish - Fresh Tuna, Marlin, Red Snapper, I felt like we were the King and Queen every day and really got to begin to appreciate how well you are treated when you have money to spend. It does help, indeed.

Yet, the highlight of each day was still crawling into bed with Rosie. *I will never forget waiting each night and see what kind of excitement she might have in store for me. Didn't have to be anything new every night - she had perfected so many ways to make me feel good. Sometimes it would start even before I got in bed. I'd come out of the shower, and she'd be laying under the covers, but as I approached the bed, she'd reach out and touch and caress me and I would once again be completely under her spell. She'd seduce me in wonderful ways every night - with touches, feeling and kisses all over my body, and then invite me to do the same to her. I now knew every part of her body, yet she could turn around in the most wonderful ways to cuddle up to me and take full advantage of touching me intimately in every spot - softly at first, then her hands would hold me more firmly -   I could never dream of anything better than what we had together at that time. Who ever thought that things could eventually go so wrong!*

Now I was getting tired. I looked at my watch and saw that it was 3:00 AM - still time enough to get into bed and see if I could sleep. With all my memories of Rosie and our sex life, I felt as if I missed her dearly, or was it just that I was slightly aroused by memories and longed for a soft body next to me. I did fall asleep and slept well until morning.

Part 2

Chapter 8

DAY TWO - CHECKING THINGS OVER

I was amazed that I finally had gotten some good sleep. I showered again, got dressed and made myself some breakfast. Just toast, juice and coffee, but it really tasted good. I figured I had better be ready for whatever may happen today. Somehow, I figured that Ella's body would not have been discovered yet, but I knew I had to be ready for when they would break the news to me. I got back into the comfortable recliner with another cup of hot coffee, and my thoughts drifted back to the death scene in Ella's condo. I smiled at that recollection and started reconstructing the crime in my head. I knew I had the timing all figured out and the time was right.

It was on Friday night, February 17th, I went up to Ella's place. I knew that she was meeting a friend and going out for dinner that night, so I would have time working for me. - Luckily this time of year, it got dark early, what with Daylight Savings Time and all, so I had darkness on my side. Quickly when I knew no one was looking, I entered her security code and slipped inside. I then went to the kitchen and out the back door - one of her golf clubs from the back closet in hand. At this time of day there was a lot of traffic going by that made considerable noise - in fact Ella had complained about it and was considering moving to a quieter area, but for now it was helping my plan a great deal. I deliberately broke the kitchen window. I wanted the police to think it was an interrupted robbery that had caused her murder. This was at exactly 5:30. Oh yes, I had everything perfectly timed. I reset the security system. I took off my overcoat and carefully set it on the sofa. I wanted to be sure that I would have full arm movement and not take any chances of missing my mark. Hitting the right spot was of crucial importance. I had taken the plastic bag out from my inside coat pocket that contained the old surgical gown and put it on. I already had my gloves on that I had worn while I was walking over - it was after all pretty cold out and I just kept them on through all of the rest of the time - especially when I took the golf club and broke the window.

That was a tricky part - There was a yard guard light in back of the condo building which sort of lit up the back area. Ella had many times complained about that as when she was in her robe in the evening and decided that she'd like a snack, she felt uncomfortable turning on the light in the kitchen because anyone who happened to be outside would have easily seen her walking around. I had laughed and told her she'd better just be careful not to walk around in the nude, but she still had me put up a shade so that she could pull it down if she wanted more privacy. At any rate, I walked slowly, staying close to the building, watching to make sure no one would see me there. I broke the window with the club - right where I could reach in and unlock the window and raise it up, leaving an entry space big enough to crawl into. Then when I went back inside, I put the club back in the closet. I did remember to knock things over, including knocking over a plant that she had by the sink so that it made a mess, think I actually made it look like someone had indeed crawled into the kitchen

Now everything was set for the final step. I walked back into the living room,

I reached up and loosened the bulb in the fixture inside the door so it wouldn't light up when she turned the switch. Yes, all of this had to be done perfectly. I knew enough about her to feel sure that she would not bother to find out if the bulb was really burned out, it would just be another thing that she would put on her list for me to take care of next time she had me over for dinner. Then the stage was set. I had a small flashlight with me, but I didn't want to use it if it wasn't necessary. There was a street light outside which provided enough light for me to see my way to the kitchen.

Once there, I found the drawer where I knew she kept the knives and used the flashlight to find the best carving knife that she had. Who knew better than me? I had carved many a roast or turkey for her over the years. I had deliberately gone out and checked it last time I was over - making an excuse that next time she felt like it, a good beef roast would sure taste wonderful. I even suggested that maybe she'd be kind enough to invite both Lola and I over, and I'd make sure the knife was ready so I could properly carve it for us. That meant a few swipes back and forth with the sharpener, especially towards the tip of it. I gave out a few compliments on what a good cook she was and maybe she could give Lola some good tips. That pleased her.

Now there were just a few minutes to go. I gripped the knife in my hand, cautiously walked back into the living room. I put the flashlight back into my pocket so I wouldn't by any chance leave it behind. I knew that when the light didn't work, she would simply walk out to the kitchen and, those would be her last steps. I stepped over towards the corner of the room by the closet and waited - moments ticking by.

Not only had I planned all of what would go on in that condo, I had even taken care of the only possible other complication. I had considered that the couple who lived upstairs from Ella may have heard any raucous that may have made suspicious noises.

I was a friend of theirs also, and I had given them some tickets for a good play which was showing down town, telling them that I had another commitment and wouldn't be able to use them. They had thanked me profusely for the tickets, and I, secretly, had thanked them for taking them. I had also gone over at 2:55 in the afternoon and seen them leave the house at 3:08. That was just as I had planned. They were going to the 4:00 performance and planned on going out for a bite to eat after and certainly wouldn't be home until at least 8:00.

I was just feeling the sharp edge of the knife once more when I heard the click of the lock in the door. Suddenly I stopped breathing - I was scared. I felt panic right then. Through all of my planning, I had never planned on that. Think of it, I was scared - just like a little kid in grade school. I remember thinking, *get hold of yourself Bill, take a deep breath, soon it will be over. Yes, she tried the light - said "Oh dam" but closed the door behind her. I heard the click of her high heels on the tile in the entryway, then, via the light coming in the windows from the street light, I saw her slowly making her way into the kitchen. As she went to snap on the light, I saw a bit of her gray wool skirt and I heard myself laugh hysterically as I lunged forward and plunged the knife forcefully and deep, penetrating the soft flesh of this human mortal.*

I remember crouching over her for a moment; just long enough to see the knife lodged in her throat. Her eyes stared up at me with a pathetic look of horror in them, and I barely heard her whisper "Why?" Now the deep red blood was running down her white blouse. The photographer in me wished that I could have taken pictures of that wonderful contrast - red on white on top of her gray skirt, and still those horror- stricken eyes looking straight at me. It would have been perfect composition. Next, I heard what people call the gurgle of death emerging from her lungs. Then all that was left was the blood softly pouring over on to the floor.

I then carefully took off the surgical gown and gloves. Next, I walked cautiously around her body, avoiding stepping in any blood, I didn't want to take a chance on getting any on my shoes. This day of age with all of the forensic science procedures they seem to have come up with, I knew that I had to be extremely careful while I carried off every step along the way. I went back to the hall and stowed the gown and gloves in the bag and stuffed it back in my coat pocket. After that was done, I put my regular gloves on, and opened her purse which she had set on the deacons bench next to the door. She always thought it was handy to have it there, as some of the few friends that she had were getting older, and it was convenient for them to have the bench there so that when they came in, especially in the winter of course, they could sit down and take off or put on their boots to face the snow and ice. I remembered when she got it - of course she had asked me my opinion as she did with most everything, and I obliged and told her I thought it would be just the one she needed and wanted. At any rate, I took the purse, poured out the contents and took the money out of her billfold being rather messy as I was doing it so that it would look like I was really in a hurry.

I couldn't believe to see how my hands were shaking. Oh well, that too shall pass. Next, I opened some drawers in the buffet in the dining room where I knew she kept a fair amount of cash - of course I messed them all up so the police would think I just made a lucky find. I knocked some things off of a couple of shelves, and that too was just setting the right picture. The final step was to reset the security system and safely leave the scene of the crime.

That was when I finally took my gloves off and put them in the plastic bag which I then sealed and put in the overcoat pocket and finally put my coat on. I buttoned it up as calmly as possible, went through the kitchen - only looking over towards the body to make sure that I didn't step in any blood and went out the back door. Carefully I again walked around the building making sure that no one was in sight and eased back out to the sidewalk and down the street. It was done - it was over, and I'd really done it. I think all went very well.

❧

Chapter 9

TIME TO TRY AND STAY CALM

Being as I was sure that no one would discover what had happened to Ella at least for a day or two. I had to concentrate on just relaxing and think about pleasant things. I debated about just what to do to make my day seem like any other weekend day. Normally I would have been spending time with Lola, but she was gone for the weekend - spending some time with some old college friends. That's another reason why I had picked this time to take care of the Ella matter, Lola wouldn't be with me - just in case I had a bout with nerves or anything.

Lola had entered into my life about 2 years ago. Let's see - Rosie and I had been married for only about a year when Mac died. It was a surprise to everyone. He'd always seemed to be in such good health, he made sure that he ate pretty well, exercised - was out hiking a lot, but of course as I said before, he was a Type A person. When things went wrong at work, he'd hit the roof, and all hell would break loose for everyone. There would be board meetings called, lots of yelling, and occasionally whomever may be to blame for what didn't go right, ended up out of the company, and quickly. I had learned a long time ago to try and stay neutral on everything - just concentrated on keeping the books all in order, and never voiced an opinion unless it concerned finances and Mac asked specific questions. This type of behavior never got better, only worse.

When I got more into the family, I saw that the home life was getting worse also.

I don't know how Mac and Ella had managed to stay together as long as they did and had hit that magic Golden Anniversary + 1 more year, but things definitely had gotten even more tense. Ella was chipping away at him all of the time, and he wasn't just ignoring the remarks any more. Some of his retorts to her had indeed become rather sharp, which surprised me, and I think Rosie was feeling some of the hurt also.

Thus, it was that after one of the big Conner's gala parties - probably aggravated by Mac having too much to drink, all hell broke loose. Everyone else had left, but Rosie and I were still there, and a few remarks from Ella put Mac into a tirade - he started yelling and swearing like I'd never heard him carry on before. He even went over to the bar and started smashing glasses. Rosie asked me to please make him stop. I tried talking to him, but that made him even angrier, and frankly I was getting sort of scared. I felt that if he would have had a gun around right then, he probably would have started shooting. Then suddenly he grabbed at his chest - got a terrible look on his face and fell flat to the ground. Ella, Rosie and I all stood in shock for a few seconds. I finally yelled "Rosie, call 911" and I went over and knelt down next to him, but I think he was dead already. I didn't know if I should roll him over or even touch him. I didn't know how to do CPR and had heard tales that sometimes untrained persons could do more damage than good by trying and not doing things right. Rosie and Ella were both screaming, and Ella was crying uncontrollably. Rosie did get to the phone and called 911. After getting the information they said help was on the way. It seemed like ages before the Police and the Ambulance got there, but I'm sure it was probably not too long, of course the Conner's place was not exactly in the middle of the city, so it was a few miles away from help also.

They did all the heroic stuff they could, but nothing seemed to help. They did get him into the ambulance, but I saw a couple of the guys shaking their heads. I quickly got Ella and Rosie into my car and followed the ambulance, but it was only a few minutes after they got him into the ER that they came out and informed us that he was dead. Truly the end of an era at the Conner company, but Rosie was there.

Chapter 10

THE NEW BOSS

Yes, a couple of weeks after the funeral, Rosie became the head CEO. I knew she was well qualified, as did everyone else in the company. All of the officers and everyone on the board were familiar with her and her way of thinking was pretty much the same as had been her fathers. She did put some new programs to work within the company, and I felt that most of them were good steps in the right direction. Computer programming by this time was of course really big business, and getting most competitive, so she had to be aware of what all of the companies were doing, and she kind of put me in charge of keeping track of that. It was a big job, and I don't think that she really thought I was doing a good enough job. She started harping at me just like Ella used to do with Mac. "For pity sake, Bill - didn't you see what was going on over there?" "Bill, you've got to make more of an effort." "Bill, why didn't you tell me that we needed more financial help on that program?" "Bill, this is serious - you'd better start giving me more reports." Thank heavens she didn't go through all of this routine when the other employees were around - no, she saved all of it just to bug me and reprimand me like I was a little kid. I suddenly wasn't quite so happy with her as I had been. Even the sex life couldn't compensate for the anger I was beginning to feel about all of it. What sex life there was any more, she was now too tired - had too many things that she had to get reports out on and figuring out the agenda for the monthly board meetings. Living with a top executive was not quite as much fun as living with the bosses daughter. I was always expected to have the financial records in my head so I could answer anything about the company. I admired her for her abilities, but I was becoming rather disenchanted when I thought about how many years this was going to go on. I could also see that she was getting more and more stressed out, and her temper was getting shorter all of the time.

I could tell that other employees were not exactly enjoying having her as the top executive anymore, but I had to admit she was raking in lots of business, and the financial outlook of the company was better than it had ever been. Rosie did one thing to keep everyone who worked for her happy - she rewarded them with salary increases and bonuses whenever it was called for. Obviously, all employees will forgive many other short comings when their own monetary needs are taken care of. In that aspect, she was considered a wonderful boss. They didn't have to go home with her at night.

This behavior went on - getting worse all of the time. Then one night when we were over having dinner with Ella, Rosie started talking about work and a work project that Conner's had been involved with which was starting to go bad, and Rosie was sure that she was going to lose the account. She had been raving on about this for a couple of weeks. Everyone started shaking in their boots now when Rosie started ranting and raving - feeling it was Mac all over again. Well, that's what she started doing that night.

Ella hadn't seen much of this behavior before, and I know she was stunned. She tried to quiet her down, which made things worse. I finally calmed her down and convinced her that we'd better go home. This damn ranting and raving was finally getting to be too much for me. We had only been married for 5 years, but I began to get stronger and stronger feelings that I couldn't hack it any more. I actually talked to Ella, telling her all of my feelings, and finally admitting that I was serious about breaking things off with Rosie. I honestly thought it better for both Rosie and me if the marriage were over.   Ella was, amazingly, almost on my side. She had come back into the scene at the company occasionally in the next couple of years and had seen what was happening there. I don't know if she had ever talked to Rosie about it - I know Rosie never said anything.

Our home life was getting more and more hectic, and I could see the looks on the other employees faces - ones that I knew well, and it was becoming humiliating for me to have to try and put on smiles and greet them as I had for many years, so I finally gave up. I asked Rosie for a divorce. She was furious at first, but finally she calmed down and admitted that she just couldn't act the role of a loving wife while she was holding down the job of a full time CEO, and I guess I came out second on the list. Keeping Conner's up and running and competitive in the Computer world was her real first and probably only love. Finally, shedding a few tears, she said that it would perhaps be the best thing to do, as she was not ready to give up her career or Mac's company. I asked her if she wanted me to quit work, but that didn't seem to fit into the picture as she didn't trust anyone with the books as much as she trusted me, so somehow, we agreed that we would be able to just be boss and employee and I'd just keep doing the best job I could. We didn't run into problems with it - in fact hardly had time to. I moved out of the Town Home we had lived in and found a nice little apartment - not too far from Ella's, which I had always thought was in a most convenient location.

Chapter 11

I JUST COULDN'T TAKE
IT ANYMORE

Most everyone at work didn't seem to be shocked when they found out that we were getting divorced. A couple of guys whom I had known for many years, even said they admired the fact that I had put up with Rosie for as long as I did, as they saw the nastier sides of her. I, on the other hand knew the passionate and loving side of her, which led me to ignore other behaviors I suppose. They were a bit surprised that I was staying on, wondering if it wasn't going to be difficult to be in the same working environment together. I assured them that we didn't hate one another, and I respected her as being the head CEO, and she respected me for keeping all of the financial records straight and wanted me still to be the financial adviser. I of course was not really close to any of the other employees, especially since Rosie and I were married - guess they were afraid that any "over coffee talk and gossip" would very likely be carried back to Rosie in after dinner conversations. I think I could have restrained, but it really was better for me not to have to hide anything - the good old 'what you don't know won't hurt you' adage, and I could live with that.

Rosie had really been very kind when it came to divorce settlements - of course I was fearful of what the outcome would be for that, but being as she was in a high tax bracket already, and as comfortably solvent that most people could ever hope to be, she never talked about any alimony, or talk of splitting up assets, etc. She even agreed to a simple, non - contested divorce - hired an attorney to draw up all of the legal papers - vowing to me that she would like to keep good working relationships, and also friendships, if possible. Yes, it was surprisingly easy - perhaps I took it a little harder than I had anticipated. Our divorce had only been finalized for seven months when things took a very surprising end.

Ella took the divorce very hard and wanted to try and remain friends with me.

That was fine, but there were times when she would pull dinners or meetings at her place. Sometimes with other people from work, but always including Rosie, which got to be rather uncomfortable. One night, with 3 other people from the board over for dinner, the conversation got extremely heated. Things were sort of in a slump at work, but I didn't feel that it had much to do with the business or any of the employees, it was just that the economy was in a downward trend. In fact, the headlines most every night were based on the economy - unemployment - people losing jobs they'd had for years, forcing many to lose their homes. Even if they considered selling their big homes and move into smaller ones, the housing market was so bad that they wouldn't be able to sell them anyhow. Yes, the majority of employees at Conner's were getting pretty worried, but we hadn't had to lay off anyone so far. The stock market was on a roller coaster ride every day, but lately it had been taking more dips than rises. Rosie was getting scared, but being Rosie, who never would show any fear for anything, she just became belligerent. I had tried to assure her that I felt Conner's would be OK, but I did tell her that perhaps the big expansions that she had planned should be put on hold for a while. That was not what she wanted to hear. Through all these now many years, even though the economy had sometimes rocked a bit, Conner's had thrived. Yes, she was spoiled. I suppose it wasn't all just that she felt scared and uncertain if she was doing a good enough job, she was preserving the memory of her father, and she had always adored and admired him and was happy that he had confidence enough in her to train her in as the inheritor of his company. Well, it finally all came to a head, and in the presence of others.

CAROL JOAN CAMPBELL

Chapter 12

THE ECONOMIC PICTURE TAKES ITS TOLL

What set the scene that night was when some of the people at the dinner table started expressing their concerns for what was going to happen. Rosie started acting like a trapped animal. It probably was because she didn't have any concrete answers that she could come up with, so she started giving really angry responses. The whole thing was becoming one big mess. Ella was shocked and dismayed, but she took hold. She finally asked everyone to please leave, go home and cool off and we'd have some answers for them the next day. They hurriedly obliged and we thought it was over. Rosie didn't though - she took that action as further fuel adding to the fire that was burning inside of her. By now she was flushed and yelling at both Ella and me. Ella was now crying hysterically, and I didn't know who to attend to first.

I was afraid that I was going to have to physically restrain Rosie - it was a nightmare.

She was acting just the way Mac had the night he had died, and in just a few minutes the scene with Mac was reenacted, but this time it was Rosie who fell to the floor. I remember yelling "No, it can't be a heart attack, women don't have heart attacks," but there she was, gasping, holding her chest and crying and moaning horribly.

This time I was the one who ran to the phone and called 911 - they tried to tell me what to do to try CPR - Ella, who was still sobbing horribly and I both worked on her while we waited for professional help, but nothing seemed to change, in fact things just seemed to get worse and soon I was hearing Rosie making that terrible sound - the gurgle of death, and I knew it had ended. When the police and paramedics arrived and assessed what had happened, they pronounced her dead at the scene.

I was in for another big surprise after Rosie died. She had taken care of so many of the fine details about Conner's - such as being sure that one of the other directors on the board had been designated to become head CEO if anything should happen to her, but that Ella remain on the board and any big decisions had to be approved by her. She also had designated that I remain on the board and as an advisory consultant even after my retirement, stating that my record had always been impeccable and my honestly was greatly admired by all. High compliments from an employer, and a former wife. There was, however one detail that she had forgotten. She had a personal life insurance policy - the two million dollar one that she had taken out after we were married. She had put me down as the sole benefactor, and she had never changed it. I was shocked - most pleasantly, but I felt sort of guilty about collecting it. I had even brought it up to Ella, but she said that I should just accept it and do as I pleased with the money. I did give to several charities and set up a Scholarship fund at Rosie's college designating that it be called Rosie Connor's Scholarship fund, which pleased Ella greatly. I of course placed much of it in good investments and was confident that I was set comfortably for life.

Again, within 5 years, Conner's had lost their CEO. The doctor said it was a massive heart attack, and that if she would have survived, she would never have been able to live the life style that she had become accustomed to. Her doctor later informed us that he knew that she had been having some really bad heart problems, probably hereditary, but she had never divulged any of that information to me. That's perhaps why she never wanted to get pregnant. I thought she was just being stubborn and enjoying the role of the business world and that it was selfish. I would have liked to have children like my brothers. Susie was doing fine - in spite of not having any kids, and in reality, Rosie and I were also - yet there was a yearning. Now I finally realized that perhaps she had other reasons - if only she would have shared that with me. At this stage in my life I had fully accepted that I was getting too old to become a parent - wouldn't really be fair to start another generation - I was getting close to 60. Better to just prepare for retirement, but then I met Lola.

Chapter 13

THE SUNSHINE AFTER THE STORM

Suddenly the phone rang, rather startling me. I answered it, and it was Lola. I was so surprised to hear her voice "Hi Bill, just thought I'd check in and see if you were missing me". I answered, "Of course I am - just sitting here thinking about you and wondering if you're having a good time". "We're all having a blast" she replied, "but thought I'd let you know that I probably may not be back until late tomorrow evening, so I don't think that I'll have a chance to meet you for dinner like I thought I might. We're meeting up with another gal who couldn't make it today, so we're going to have dinner with her - OK?" "Sure" I answered - "Glad you're having a good time, and guess I'll just have to live without you until Monday - give me a call when you get back and I'll take you out for dinner and get all of the gossipy news about everyone when we're together". She laughed and said "That sounds super - love you - see you then. Bye-Bye."

That was a pleasant surprise, and probably would help things work out better anyhow. It did remind me though about that beautiful blue dress in Wright's window. I put on my coat - got into the car, driving around a bit first to enjoy a fresh coating of snow that had covered the ground and drove to the shopping center and bought the new dress for Lola. The snow was an added surprise, not very much - just a covering, but it would be enough to cover up any remnants of footprints which might have been spotted when the police finally started checking things out. I stopped at the McDonald's on the way back - picked up a Big Mac, some French fries and a Chocolate Milk Shake and headed back to my comfortable and most peaceful apartment.

My relationship with Ella was probably sort of strange as far as a lot of people were concerned. I always got along just fine with her and Mac even before Rosie and I were married. Being a part of the company, I knew what was going on, and I knew that they relied upon me and gave me full responsibilities in handling all of the company finances, and I did a good job for them. Never was tempted to change any figures for my benefit or anyone else's either. Mom and Dad had taught me that honesty was a top quality in whatever career I may follow, and I believed that and respected them for always being honest, so I knew it was just the way to be. They showed me how they felt both by paying me a decent wage and treating me quite well.

Now, after Rosie died, Ella began to treat me like an only child - taking the place of the one that she had lost under such tragic circumstances. I know that even when Rosie and I were going through the divorce proceedings, Ella seemed to blame Rosie for our broken marriage more than it being any fault of mine. That made it easier for me to deal with all of our acquaintances who also knew Ella, Lola being one of them.

Ella never required much of me, so it was simple just to go over and enjoy a good meal once a week and in return, I would help with a few chores around her condo - putting up new curtains, hanging pictures, fixing a drippy faucet, etc.

Some things really bugged me though - there was still the constant picking about things. I know I'd seen how she was with Mac, but I was so in love with Rosie that I ignored when people tried to warn me. If I ever said anything to anyone they would just laugh and say "like mother like daughter". I never found that very amusing. Now I seemed to get really uncomfortable about the criticisms that Ella was always throwing out - just like Rosie had done - sit up straight - don't bite your nails - comb your hair again - don't wear that tie, it looks terrible - you need a new suit - smile more - don't talk so much - try and keep up an interesting conversation, etc.

Luckily, it wasn't every time we were together that she harped so bad, because many times she included some other of her friends over. Occasionally it was another couple, and then we would end up the evening with playing 500, or sometimes even Bridge. I had known how to play 500 - Mom and Dad had taught me that, as they did all of us kids, and many times when we were over, we would take turns playing with them. They really loved to play games, both board games and card games, but never wanted anything to do with playing for money. Casinos were forbidden territory as far as they were concerned. They never would wager any money for even small bets, and poker was not enjoyment to Dad, actually a thing to be feared. Oh yeah, he liked to sing that song *"You've got to know when to hold, know when to fold"* but just liked the sound of it, not the real content of the words. Here I go again - sliding back into the past and remembering so many things about growing up. Guess it was a pleasant part of my life, and always made me even more nostalgic about old times. It seemed to present a comfort zone to me and my Psychologist, just one that I visited occasionally when I felt tendencies to think about too many strange things – I knew then that I just had to talk about it a while, and she would focus me back to full reality and assure me that I wasn't flipping out again.

Back to Ella's friends - some of them were just endurable, but some were really wonderful and interesting, especially Lola, now she was a real gem. She had really been a friend of Rosie's so I had known her for a while also. But Ella had known her since she was a teenager, the girls had gone to school together. Lola had gotten married while she was going to college, but things hadn't worked out too well. I believe I heard that she had even worked at Conner's for a short time, but that was before my time with the company.

Chapter 14

A MOST PLEASANT CHAPTER IN MY LIFE

Guess that Ella must have seen some extra spark from both of us after we'd been in one another's company a few times, as Ella would invite her many times when she also had me over, and we were able to converse comfortably both with each other and with Ella. I got a little uncomfortable sometimes when the talk would turn to Rosie, but of course I realized that she had been familiar company for both of them in times gone by. Ella was actually the one who set up our first date. She had tickets to a special play that was showing down town. As far as Broadway shows were concerned, this was a spectacular musical, but an old time one, "Showboat". Ella said that she had seen it more than once and asked if we had. Both Lola and I admitted that we hadn't. We seemed to know some of the old songs from it, but never the whole production, so she suggested that perhaps the two of us could attend together, and that seemed to make good sense. In fact, I took it one step further and asked Lola if she would care to have dinner with me before the play, and I was pleasantly surprised when she said, "That would be very nice, thanks and I'll be looking forward to it". She had such a pretty voice, and I found myself really looking forward to it. We had a wonderful time that evening. I had asked her what kind of restaurant she wanted to go to, and she stated that she really liked both Chinese and Italian quite well". I was happy to hear her make actual suggestions, instead of a fake 'wherever you take me, or I don't really care' answer. Always thought that was sort of a cop out. I also had been used to all of the Conner's - Mac, Ella and Rosie who always had a definite answer, and I have to admit, after being around them for a few years, I really admired that quality, and gained much more confidence in myself by also giving definite answers.

I somehow thought perhaps Italian would be nicer - a cheerier atmosphere, candles on the table - pleasant music playing in the background, and just basic good food. Sure, I might add - possibly a little more romantic. I knew of Maurice's that had a good reputation, and they even had a couple of Italian waiters who would occasionally break out in some Italian songs too, so it was fun also. I picked her up early, as I didn't want to have to be in any big hurry to get to the play. I wanted time to enjoy a couple of glasses of wine both before and during our meal. It was a perfect dinner. I hadn't had such an enjoyable time since I had dated Rosie.

Well, we went on to the play - barely getting there on time, as the wine had become a little too enjoyable, and it was tough to break away and catch a taxi. The play was fantastic, and of course we both remembered lots of songs, but it suddenly brought on some most interesting and delightful feelings as the actress sang.

"Just My Bill, an Ordinary Guy" and Lola put her hand over mine and gave it a little squeeze. I felt a tingling that I hadn't felt since the divorce - it was a sexy gesture to me. I had advanced and put my arm around her, and we comfortably sat enjoying the rest of the play, but happily cozied up to one another. That music from Showboat was imbedded in my heart from there on in. I even bought 2 CD's of the music that was on sale in the entrance of the theatre before we left that night. How she smiled when I handed one to her - I know I really looked at her then, and she was beautiful.

OK, let's get back to the plan and Ella, I have to keep all of this information in its proper order - what to tell the police if necessary, and what things I should be careful to mention. I probably wouldn't have taken it for so long, but things got a bit more interesting when she finally asked me to help her with her finances. It had been quite a revelation to me to see just how well off she was. I knew that she never seemed to need for anything, but she always seemed to live towards the frugal end of life these days rather than splurging. I had no idea of the wealth involved.

The company was going along quite well, and Ella confided in me that she had someone who had contacted her about a takeover, and she was considering it. She had insisted that I be a part of the board of Conner's, which provided me with a nice salary. She had hired another accountant so he could learn procedures from me. I was still getting an extremely generous salary and I didn't have to spend long hours in the office. As time passed by, I can't say that I was very important to the company, but it gave me the time and money to enjoy a special pass time that I had always loved - photography, and I was loving it.

Chapter 15

HAPPY DIVERSIONS

Nothing made me happier than when Lola and I would spend time together on the weekend. No matter what the weather was like, I always begged her to have some time which I called "Shot's for My Album" time. I'd think of some beautiful background scenery - be it a zoo, a botanical garden, just a down town scene, etc., and I'd take pictures, of course I had a fantastic model with me to pose in so many of the pictures. Sometimes I'd even choose a location that would fit with whatever color outfit she would have on, and it always seemed to work.

The new digital cameras were so fantastic - I could just keep on shooting and filling up a whole memory stick if I wanted to and know I'd have the joy of loading them on to the computer, delete what I wanted to, edit what I wanted to and print out the pictures. I began to fill the walls in the den/computer room with Nature and Lola - an unbeatable combination. Lola never got annoyed with me when I wanted to take her pictures, in fact she rather enjoyed it. Yes, that definitely made things advanced in other areas. I'll never forget the first time we had sex.

She had come over to my place where I had invited her for dinner, telling her that I had some new pictures to show her. She had insisted that she would make a cheese cake for dessert, and who could resist that. I had just gotten a couple of steaks to do on the grill - knew that I was pretty good at that, and just had some salad with it that I had picked up at the deli oh yeah, guess I picked up a couple of rolls to go with it, and figured that was plenty, which it was. It was a great meal, even if I do say so myself. I had started the coffee pot brewing while we ate, so while I cleared the table, Lola served up generous pieces of her raspberry cheesecake. It was marvelous, and I raved a lot all the while that we were slowly enjoying it and sipping our coffee.

After, I asked her to come in my den to see the latest pictures. I had enlarged many of the best ones and had fixed up some of the track lighting so that they would shine down on them, and it was quite a display. I know she was impressed - even shed a couple of tears as she got sort of emotional about it. I then asked her if she would let me take some pictures of just her, not worrying about locations, and she agreed. I set up a stool and got my tripod out and started focusing on her. After a couple of close-up shots, I asked her if she would unbutton her blouse a bit so it would present a better neckline. She let me unbutton it and arrange it. For the next picture I arranged it differently, unbuttoning one more button and pulling it slightly over one shoulder so that her flesh showed up more. She was wearing a deep blue blouse that looked so lovely with her blue eyes and blonde hair, but now her beautiful creamy pink skin was accented even more surrounded with the loosely flowing blue material. I couldn't stand it anymore. Next time I walked over to her, I put my arms around her, lifted her to a standing position and kissed her like I had never kissed her before, and she returned the passion by running her tongue over my lips, inviting me to open my lips and feel that tiny pink tongue gently explore my tongue and she pressed herself against me. I looked down at her, caressing her shoulders as I did and said, "Do you want to lie down in bed?", and amazingly she nodded her head up and down and held my hand as we walked into my bedroom.

This sex was far different from what I had ever had with Rosie - Lola was gentle, but teasingly wonderful. She undressed in front of me - slowly, carefully laying her clothes at the foot of the bed, then she undressed me - slightly touching each part of bare skin as she disclosed it. I hardly had to move at all, just lying down on the bed and arching a bit when she took my trousers and shorts off. Then she crawled on the bed and looked at me and started to run her fingers across all of my body, almost kneading me with both hands across my chest, down my arms, then over my hips - down the outer part of my legs, then up on the inner part of my legs and thighs. By now I desperately wanted more, but it was so tantalizing that I wanted the feel to go on forever, so I tried to slow myself down.

Then she got up on her knees and pulled my face between her soft, wonderful breasts, and gently just swayed back and forth a bit, making her breasts press against me with almost an undulating quality. I then couldn't help but make some gestures - I held her breasts in my hands and gently kissed them, and felt her nipples enlarge as I searched for them with my mouth and kissed them, and they tasted wonderful. They were not sumptuous breasts, but beautifully shaped. They were firm, but the skin was incredibly soft - I couldn't hold myself much longer, and I guess she knew it.

She suddenly rolled over, stretched herself with her arms up over her head and her legs opened to invite me in. Oh, she was as primed for me as it would ever be. I tried to control myself to get into her gently, which I did, but as she automatically started to make more inviting motions, I had to get into her as deeply as I could. I put my arms around her, holding her up against me and it only took me a couple of deep lunges and I came. She started crying, which shattered me. I was afraid that I had hurt her, and held her tight, saying "I'm sorry darling - I didn't want to hurt you", and started pulling myself away, but she held on to me tight and said "No, just stay there, I only cried because it felt so wonderful". The evening was beautiful, gentle, but most fulfilling.

When we separated and laid back on the bed, I found that I felt a contentment that I had never felt before, I felt adored, and in turn, I adored Lola. She never went home that night. My new life had begun, my darling Lola and I had become one, and I knew that this would be a new chapter in my life. A new excitement, but also a new calmness came over me. I had a beautiful new companion, and my mission in life was going to be centered around showing her how she had enriched my life, and that I wanted to share whatever life I may have left to pleasing and loving her.

Before long, Ella knew that we were becoming more than just enjoying one another's company over there for dinner or an occasional movie and dinner, and she seemed to truly be happy for us. I finally told her that I felt lucky that she had introduced me to Lola and that we seemed compatible, and I really enjoyed being with her. Ella then gave me what I took as her blessing. She said that she had always enjoyed being with Lola also, and hoped that all of us could continue to be friends. She also went on to say that she hoped I wouldn't mind too much if she would still occasionally ask me to help her with certain things, stating - "You've always been very good to me, and I just want you to know that I appreciate it, but I don't want to be a burden to you." I assured her that I was honored to be trusted by her, and I certainly didn't mind helping. True, I had helped with small things around the house, and the favors had begun to increase, but I wasn't about to stop. In fact, when she had asked me to help her with her finances, I was extremely surprised, but most willing. It had been quite a revelation to me to see just how well off she was. I had no idea of the wealth involved before I saw it all in black and white. Luckily, Mac had set aside plenty to provide for her in the event of an untimely death and the company was continuing to thrive. I must admit that when I had found that all of this money was available, I no longer had a shred of guilt about hanging on - she continued doing special things for me and even gave me unexpected gifts, which had surprised me. I used to make protests, but as they continued on, I began to feel that she was thoroughly enjoying doing it, and I started just more and more accepting them as graciously as I could and letting her know how much I appreciated all that she did for me.

Now I knew that she had more than she could ever spend. The sad thing was that there were no remaining relatives to share all of this with after she was gone. Oh well, she had many charities that she planned to divide it with - everything from a Cancer Research project to the local Animal shelter. I knew that she gave annually a very large sum of money to the Heart Association, a natural what with losing both Mac and Rosie to heart attacks, and I admired her for that. She had chaired a couple of fund-raising events for them that had increased their research projects by almost a million dollars, and she was honored by the society for her leadership and participation.

She had even been featured in the local newspaper when she was chosen as the Senior Citizen of the year for all her volunteer work at the Senior Citizen Center, and her generous donations of both money and time to head the various organizations fund raising activities. She was indeed well known and respected by the community. I knew that her death would have an impact on many of those organizations, but I also had a plan - after the proper times had elapsed and when I was sure of the financial situations, I would step in and pronounce my willingness to keeping all of the good works going in Ella's and Rosie's memory, and keeping the Conner's name honored. There may be a few things of my own, so that I would become as well respected by all of the organizations, and they would welcome me into the inner circle of the societies benefactors.

What really peaked my interest however was that while searching through all of her financial papers, I found a copy of a life insurance policy for $10 million dollars, and the beneficiary was Rosie, but with the stipulation that if anything happened to her, the money went on to ME. Well, that narrowed it down - that now meant that it would all come to me - no strings attached. Not too shabby!!! It was then that I figured it was not too bad to play the role of the good guy and make at least weekly trips to spend time with her just to keep up a good front. I don't know if she realized that the copy of the policy had been with the other papers or not, but I wasn't about to bring it up, and she never did either. All her harping never diminished, however and I knew that it was going to get to be more than I could bear before too long.

Poor Mac, I don't know how he had put up with the nit picking on a day to day basis for all their married life - if indeed it had always been like that. Maybe it came on gradually - I doubt that she was probably like that when they first got married, as I truly think that they shared a great love for one another. I suppose it maybe got worse as Mac became more successful - didn't spend as much time with her - had more stresses at work. She did lots of entertaining, etc. It probably wasn't just the harping, but when added to all of the other elements with the daily stresses, ultimately it was his bad heart that gave out and caused the fatal heart attack. It had been only about a year and a half now since Rosie had succumbed to the same demise. Yes, probably hereditary as the Doctor had said.

Well, now they were both gone, and I couldn't help but think of poor Mac, - I suddenly thought that every time I referred to Mac, whether it was to someone else or just me thinking of him, it was always Poor Mac. I couldn't stop wondering if when they all met in the great hereafter that both Rosie and Ella would start picking on him again!!!! Guess that depends upon whether they meet in heaven or hell. Enough of those thoughts!!!

Ironic I thought, I'd never had any of those kinds of thoughts about my Mom and Dad - I always knew that Mom would be in heaven eagerly waiting for Dad. He used to paraphrase another old song "Just Laura and Me, and Baby Makes Three, We're Happy in Our Blue Heaven". I can hear him now - really, I can - that great voice and how it was filled with love when he looked at Mom. That's enough of that, Bill - don't get caught up in the past again - better shake away the voices that were entering in my head, somehow, I was having trouble erasing them, actually, I was liking the voices, they were at times most comforting. Back to reality, Bill — you have to keep your head directed to make sure that all is under control, facts in order and clear. You've got to keep your wits about you. You can't afford to make any mistakes in this stage of the game.

Chapter 16

TAKE YOUR TIME, BILL AND STAY CALM

I decided to take a little break - it was Saturday and the shops were open a little later, so thought this would be the right time to go back to Wright's and get the dress for Lola. It might begood timing, as I could verify that I had been there - have the charge slip as evidence, etc. *Good thinking, Bill.* I walked by the store again to check the window and make sure that the dress was still on display, and it was. Good - I stood there for a couple of minutes, but as thoughts began to pull up in my head, I thought I'd better just get inside. I didn't wander around, just went into the women's dress department. I explained to the clerk what I wanted, and she was happy to help me. She asked me what size I needed - I had to think about that for a bit, but then I remembered being with Lola one time when she bought something and asked for a size 12. I was proud of myself that I had remembered, but then I was finding myself placing more things about Lola in my memory so I could feel more and more familiar with everything about her.

The clerk brought it back, and it was even more classy looking at it close up than it had been in the window. It was a little more expensive than I had anticipated, but I was after all not really hurting financially, and soon I'd be able to afford anything that I wanted, and I hoped that Lola would be included. I asked the clerk where the gift -wrapping counter was, as this was a special gift. She asked if it was a birthday or anniversary or something. I chuckled and said "I wish it was for an anniversary - maybe this will help her make up her mind and we'll be celebrating an anniversary soon. "No, she's just been out of town for a while, and this is to show her how much I miss her". She smiled as she answered "After she gets this, I'm sure she'll be one happy gal. Wish my boyfriend would do something like this for me sometime!". Then after the credit slip was signed and she put it in a bag, she pointed out where the gift wrapping could be done. As I walked towards that area, I again complimented myself on choosing to do this right now. Again, it will make it known as to where I was and when I was there, which will uphold my innocence about knowing that anything had happened.

They wrapped the gift beautifully, I chose paper that had some blue tones and told them to make a big, blue bow on to decorate it. It cost $6.95 to have it done, but somehow it just seemed to top off everything just right. As I walked out of the store with the shopping bag in hand, I was very pleased both with myself and with my purchase.

Then I thought I'd just stop in at the little casual restaurant not far from Wrights. It was one that I occasionally stopped at when I just wanted to have a bite to eat. It had good food, wasn't that expensive, and better than just eating whatever I may have on hand at home and sitting by myself. As I sat down and looked at the menu, I decided that I'd go for a bowl of chili and a bread stick. That should be adequate. Besides, it was chilly outside, so may as well have some chili on the inside. What a silly thing to enter my mind - it made me smile, especially to think that I was getting away from morbid and scary thoughts, I was thinking of pleasant and funny things. *That's the way, Bill, remember, you're going to have to do some good acting in the days to come, and you'll have to learn to relax and keep under control.*

The meal tasted good, and warmed me up inside, and being in the restaurant warmed me up outside, so I was ready for the next trek back to my apartment. I asked for the check - and left a generous tip when I paid the bill. I carefully put the receipt in my billfold - more evidence that I was just acting normally, no one would see anything odd or strange from my actions. Yes, I have to be very careful of so many details. This wasn't a game - I'd have to walk that fine line on doing everything just so but trying to act as normal as possible.

I was glad to be back home - I still felt a bit chilly, so decided to start a fire in the fireplace. As I got the paper and kindling assembled, my hand kind of shook when I lit the match - yes, it dredged up memories of lighting the fire last night and having it blaze so nicely when I placed the plastic bag and what could have been evidence and watched it all go up and turn to just smoke in the chimney. *No, Bill, don't dwell on that - change your way of thinking.* OK – let's turn it around - another blazing fire will just build up some more ashes, and if any remnants could have survived last night, they would be taken care of now.

I went over to the bar and poured a little Apricot Brandy in a glass, then settled into the recliner and turned on the TV - just as well to divert my attention and not dwell on any of last night's events. I flipped through the guide button - there were some pretty good shows on tonight, but I figured that maybe a good comedy would do me the most good, so tuned in to a re-run of The Lucy Show. Couldn't go wrong with her - she'd be bound to make me chuckle a bit. At least that's what I thought but going back to that old show had more of a negative effect, I'm afraid. It once again brought me back to years ago when I was a teenager. My whole family used to sit around and watch the show together - we really enjoyed family times. Dad would pop up a big batch of popcorn - Mom had a huge bowl that she used to make bread in - really – home- made bread - *the thought of that made my mouth water.* At any rate, Dad would pop up a big double batch of popcorn, and the smell was incredible. Then when it was all popped, he'd mix up a batch of his special concoction and produce what we called "sticky popcorn". Never did get the real recipe, unfortunately, but it had butter and brown sugar and marshmallows in it. It tasted like Carmel Corn, but a little sticky (hence the name) and not crackly like lots of caramel corn was. Really hard to describe all of the qualities of it, but man did we think it was the most wonderful treat there could ever be. Susie had tried making it for us once, and it wasn't bad, but she had never gotten the exact measurements either - of course we all ate it and raved. *Gosh it's been a long time since I've been out to see Susie - I'd better call her, maybe even tomorrow and see how things are going.* She usually seems to be fine, but I'm sure she does get lonesome all by herself. That brought up some other thoughts - wonder if she is by herself or if she has found someone to share her place with? Know she's been out occasionally, but she never says much about it, so not sure. Dad's song probably would have been *"When You Come to The End of A Perfect Day". I sure have been going back to the songs - sometimes I just can hardly get them out of my mind - better watch that, Bill. Better get back to the comedy.*

Can't believe what I'm watching - that hilarious episode where Lucy and Ethel are working at the chocolate factory. I'll have to watch it really close, as I remember in some interviews which they showed after she died. They asked what her favorite episode was, and she chose this one. Not just the premise of their actions, but because a woman who actually worked in the candy factory was shown doing her job of dipping the chocolates even while Lucy and Ethel were botching everything up, and that woman never even cracked a smile - just kept on doing her job the way she was supposed to. That had really cracked up the comediennes. OK - here's the scene - they were right - she's just concentrating on doing the same old thing and not batting a glance at Lucy - funny!!

Good old memories. *What was that song - think it was back in the '50's? "Those Were The Days, My Friend, I Thought They'd Never End". OK Mitch - you've got me doing it now too.*

I did laugh through the rest of the episode. I kept the station on, but didn't even know any of the actors in the next one - guess I haven't kept up with all of the TV star - seems I'm doing well to even keep up with some good movies, and probably wouldn't even do that if it weren't for the fact that Lola really liked to go to the movies, so we did, 2 or 3 times a month. Guess I really wasn't in the mood to watch any more sitcoms, so I turned the TV off and went over and started playing some of my favorite CDs, that was really much more restful, and I had to relax.

Now it was time to plan the next day. I was getting nervous about just what was going to happen tomorrow. I figured I'd be safe today, as I didn't really think that anyone would be contacting Ella on that Friday evening or Saturday, but now I was beginning to wonder what should happen if no one else would find her. It happened often that I would go over there some time on Sunday - well, not every Sunday, but it was a contact day.

I tried to think back and remember who may have seen me on those visits, or if it was just something that I did and never thought about it. Humm - let's see. Really the only ones that I might happen to see would be the Becker's - the couple upstairs, but that wasn't every time. Her unit was a corner one, so I wasn't walking by lots of other condos to get into hers - yes, that was good. Besides, I knew that they were very involved in their church, so they probably wouldn't be around on a Sunday morning anyhow. Well, the mail person wouldn't get suspicious as yet. She had picked up her mail already on Friday - I remember seeing her put it on the table as she walked out into the kitchen, so there wouldn't be any build -up of mail in her box. She didn't subscribe to the Sunday Paper - let's see, did she have her paper with her too when she came in? *Think about it now Bill, do you remember? OK go back in time, close your eyes and concentrate.* Let's see - she entered her security number, of course I wasn't there to see her when she first opened the door - she snapped on the light, which didn't light, and then she walked slowly out to the kitchen - *think Bill* - yes, I'm sure she had the paper in her hand - she'd closed the door - where was the paper? Stop it - what's the difference - it wouldn't make any difference what she did with it - that's a stupid thing to get caught up on. Just forget it - I can't stand to go over it anymore - I must go on and figure what may happen next. *Slow down, you've got to concentrate on relaxing - take a couple of deep breaths, slowly now - there, that's better.* Let's just march on. At least I know the paper wasn't still outside of the door, and she had decided that it was silly to have the Sunday paper delivered, as she was often too busy to read it anyhow, and if she wanted one, she would pick it up at the corner convenience store. She usually ended up going down there for bread or milk or something if she needed anything on Sunday, so that had been her decision. All of this worked out fine in my plan.

Back to my coming and going - yes, it was to buy the dress and go out to eat - I have receipts, and talked to people, so think I'm safe. Let's see - what time is it? Almost 8:00 - I'd better go out and make myself something to eat - maybe just a good old peanut butter on toast. No, somehow that's not the most appealing right now. *OK, let's look in the refrigerator and see what might be lurking there. I know I should know everything, after all I'm usually the only one buying groceries and fixing myself things, but sometimes Lola would whip up something when she was over, and I was never quite sure just what that might be.*

I walked over to the fridge and when the door opened and the light went on, I'm afraid there wasn't anything too exciting to spot. Well, a little bit of milk, some butter - let's see what's down in the meat drawer, or rather what's down there that hasn't been around for too great a length of time. Looks pretty sparse, but there's a package towards the back - oh yeah, some sausage which should at least still be good - think it was just a few days ago that I got that. Well, if I just cut off a couple of slices of that and put it on a couple of pieces of bread it should taste pretty good. Oh, there's a couple of pieces of cheese too - things are looking even better. That should do. Maybe I'll make myself a cup of cocoa - sure I have some of the instant powder in the end cupboard there - yep, there were 3 packages of cocoa mix - with marshmallows, no less. This is really beginning to sound appetizing. I poured some milk in a cup and put it in the microwave to get it nice and hot. I got the sandwich made while the cocoa was heating up.   There, it does do a quick job of things. If I put it all on a dinner plate, think I can manage to get it back to the old recliner, turn on the TV and find a good movie or something. Sounds like a super comfortable evening ahead.

I flipped through a few channels and found a program on the Travel Channel which looked interesting. I always had looked at some of those places that were featured and thought how fantastic it would be to visit them. This one was on Jamaica, which looked really neat. As I watched it, it reminded me of course of Grand Cayman where Rosie and I had gone on our Honeymoon.

Chapter 17

A BACK TRACK OF MEMORIES

That had been my first overseas adventure and I had enjoyed it so much. After we were married, what with her income and mine, we certainly could have afforded to travel, but work seemed to be the thing that always interfered. We took a few short trips, but they were to Computer conventions - once to Las Vegas which had also been a first for me. I'd never even imagined that such a place existed within the good old USA. It was remarkable enough to see it when we first arrived and rode in a limo from the airport to our Hotel. We stayed at Caesar's Palace, which I guess is one of the older ones now, but I thought it was magnificent. Rosie had complained a little as she wanted to stay at Bilogios but felt that having a stay there probably wouldn't sit right with the board of Conner's - they could have figured it was a bit too extravagant. I couldn't imagine that anything could have been better than Caesar's, so I was content. We attended the conference for several hours every day but managed to get in some night life also. I'll never forget the first time we came back from the convention, I laid down for a short time well, actually, we spent some time in the Jacuzzi together, and that somehow led to some other activities. *Oh yeah, I let myself slide back to that late afternoon.*

We'd had a small bottle of champagne sent up to the room when Rosie first suggested relaxing for a bit in the Jacuzzi. It had arrived shortly in a fancy silver ice bucket along with 2 champagne glasses. The guy who delivered it asked if we'd like him to open it for us. Rosie said sure, so he did, and it had a nice pop to it. As is sometimes the procedure, he handed me the cork. I did smell it, and it had a wonderful aroma - I was never good at really identifying what all was in the fizzy wonderful liquid, but all I know is that it did smell nice. He poured a bit in a glass and handed it to me. I obliged by sipping it appreciatively and stating that it was nice. Then, tipped him generously, and when he left, I turned my attention to more interesting things. Rosie was in a playful mood. The conference had gone well - Conner's display was wonderful and inviting to everyone's eyes. That's the way Rosie looked at that moment, wonderful and inviting. She seemed to know she had my full attention and started sort of almost dancing as she slowly undressed. I think my eyes got moist - not with tears, but maybe drooling. Yes indeed, she had my full attention, and she knew it. Then she started undressing me, sliding against me while she took my tie off, was unbuttoning my shirt and unbuckling my belt and unzipping my pants. I just let them drop to the floor and started drawing her closer to me. She said "Hey, Bill - time to cool down a bit so we can enjoy being together in the Jacuzzi - they'll be plenty of time to heat up again after." What an invitation.

Well, I did as she suggested, - carried in the champagne bucket and glasses and set them on the floor next to the big tub while she was filling it up with water. After it was the right temperature, she stepped in, kneeled, turned around and smiled. She crooked her finger, inviting me to come in and join her, and that I did. We both enjoyed the feel of the warm water, and I reached over and poured us each a glass of bubbly. We must have spent an hour in there - just adding more hot water along the way and pushing the appropriate buttons to have the bubbles rise from the water and massage us in the proper areas to make us feel relaxed and wonderful. We hardly even talked. We'd turned on the radio in the other room which had a speaker sending the music into the bathroom area, so we just touched each other, drank our champagne and enjoyed each moment.

Finally, Rosie laughed and said perhaps we'd better get out or we'd both look like prunes when we went out for dinner. We got out and sort of dried one another. We then picked up the sumptuous terry cloth robes which the hotel provided and went back to the bedroom. We took off the robes and crawled into bed. We were both quite sexually worked up by all of the preceding actions, so that it didn't take too much more arousal play back and forth before I was once again inside of her, exploding in ecstasy and knowing that she had climaxed also.

Back to Vegas. When we finally had been laying there for a while, Rosie said - "Know what? I'm hungry - think I worked up a tremendous appetite" and laughed. I agreed that we'd probably better get our senses back and get dinner. After all, we had tickets for one of the big shows later that night, and I really didn't want to miss that. As we stepped out on the street, I was overwhelmed by seeing all the neon lights up and down the strip - there were signs, fountains, erupting volcanoes, animated figures, billboards telling about famous stars who were appearing. Wow - it was breath taking. I found that I could hardly take everything in. I didn't want to act like a country bumpkin, but that's sort of what I felt like at that moment.

Enough of that, Bill - you haven't had sexual thoughts about Rosie for a long time - certainly not since Lola has been around. I certainly can't start comparing them, as the sexual lives of each of them were extremely different. Yes, I had enjoyed that part of my life with Rosie to the utmost, but the tenderness of Lola was far surpassing what I had known before, and I was completely content with it. Back to the Travel Channel.

By this time, the hour on Jamaica was almost over, but I watched the sort of re-cap at the end and thought that perhaps when Lola and I got married, if she would have me that is, maybe I would suggest going to Jamaica for our Honeymoon.

I got up and carried the dishes out to the kitchen, rinsed them and put them in the dishwasher. Didn't have to run that but a couple of times a week with just me being here, but it was a good place to store them and keep the kitchen looking half way decent anyhow. I walked around a bit, went to the bathroom, and then started thinking more about what tomorrow might bring.

I was getting nervous now - what if I still didn't hear from anyone. Should I go over to Ella's pretending just to visit and discover her body? I was a bit afraid of that plan - I really didn't want to be exposed to everything there again. But if I didn't discover her, who would? I started shaking - not sure if it was shivering or just nervousness, but I didn't like the feel of it. I then did something that I hadn't done for years, I searched through the medicine cabinet and found one of my old prescription sleeping pills that I hadn't taken for a very long time but was always comforted when things started getting tense for me, to know that the bottle was there. The old use, but don't abuse - just a pill in case. This might be the pillow I needed tonight. I took a pill, drank a glass of water and crawled into bed. I turned on the clock radio, with the volume down low, not enough to really keep me awake, but loud enough to stop some of the strange thoughts which were entering my head. *The last that I remember of that night was being sure that it was my Dad singing some of those old songs on the radio, and I dreamed that he and Mom were dancing around in my bedroom.*

Chapter 18

THE NEXT STEP. DAY 3

It was Sunday Morning - I did sleep, perhaps not a deep sleep, but got sort of rested anyhow. I opened the door and picked up the Sunday Paper and went out in the kitchen and made a pot of coffee. I glanced over the front page and didn't see any shocking headlines. I didn't really think that I would, as I was sure that if Ella had been found the police would have contacted me, but still, had to check.

I made a piece of toast and poured some juice into a little glass which tasted really good. Had the toast along with my coffee while I looked briefly through the rest of the paper, but not really reading it. I was beginning to work out a plan now - thought I'd wait for a while and then call Ella well, call the condo that is. Know she wouldn't answer, but the answering machine I assumed was turned on, and I'd leave a message. That would be found, and it would be a record that I didn't know that anything was wrong. *OK - good plan, now here goes.* When I called it rang the 4 times before the message came on to leave my name and number, and I said - "Hi Ella, hope you had a good day yesterday catching up on things as you said you were going to do. Thought you may be home, but you must have decided to be a good girl and go to church this morning. Good for you. Well, if you want me to do anything for you, give me a call. Otherwise, I'll talk to you later - Bye now."

There, that went well. Now I was covered for a short time, and I'd have more time to think clearly and see where things would go from here. Now I was wishing that someone would find her soon - this waiting game really wasn't much fun. I wanted the whole thing to be over with - an end - I was getting a little fearful that things were building up inside of me, I couldn't take any chances now. Didn't really dare to go out anywhere, as I was waiting for the news. Also waiting to hear from Lola, so this was a good time to just stay inside and try to act as normal as I could.

I took a shower and got dressed in just my casual lounge type clothes, so in case anyone should happen to stop by for any reason, they would find me in my usual at home attire. But the clock was moving slowly.

I ran the dishwasher, turned on the TV and started working on the crossword puzzle in the paper. The Sunday one was always a big challenge. I really liked doing cross word puzzles - found it good to use my head and not have to think about things. That was really good right now - kept me concentrating on just words instead of what might be happening.

The Phone rang, and I almost jumped out of the chair. *Slow now, Bill, let it ring a couple of times.* I calmed myself down and then picked it up "This is a reminder that we can help you reduce your mortgage pay------" I hung up - another annoying recorded call. I know that lots of people have to make their living by making telephone calls, but I just didn't think it was right to have these recorded calls coming on Sundays. That was supposed to be a day of rest for everyone. Don't know why I even thought that. Dad after all had been a car salesman, and back in his prime he had to work on Sundays. That was a big day for car sales - couples were out together considering the purchase of a car. It worked well for him back then, as he worked for a Jewish car dealer, and there was still a lot of bigotry when it came to dealing with the Jewish people. But here was this good old Scandinavian - they'd be sure and deal with him. Dad never had a problem with any of his employers - he respected them as good people, and they were extremely good to him. All I knew was that they paid my Dad, so in turn they took care of me also. Thank goodness things have come around in the last decades, and those feelings have faded. Now back to the crossword puzzle.

It's 2:30 - now I'm getting a little nervous. I think I'll carry out a little plan that I actually thought of a couple of weeks ago - I'll call Ella again, then when there's no response, I'll call the Becker's. Yes, this might work, and so I called. "Well Hi there Lois," I said to her when she answered, "How you guys doing? Super. So, you enjoyed the play? That's great.   You're welcome, so glad that you could use the tickets. Yes, I'm fine - Lola has been gone for the weekend, so I haven't done much". I was really wondering though, I've tried to get hold of Ella a couple of times today, and wondered if by any chance you had seen her? Hmmmmm - that's strange. Oh well, guess she doesn't have to check in with me all of the time.   Well, if you see her, I would appreciate it if you'd ask her to give me a ring. I'm waiting for Lola to get back home, but I'll keep trying to catch Ella also. Bye now!"

There, that was done - pretty good cover, even if I do say so myself. May as well get a bite to eat and find something useful to do.

4:00 - The phone rang again - again I jumped - this time it was a most pleasant call though. It was Lola, and she said, "I'm running late, as usual, so don't plan on having dinner with me, but I will be in touch as soon as I get back." She said she had been having a great time, but that she could hardly wait to be with me again. Now those were most wonderful and welcome words. I had planned the whole thing with Ella based on the fact that I knew Lola would be gone - it all fit in the plan, but oh how I missed her. I really love that gal - maybe soon I'd surprise her with a diamond and a real proposal. I'd sort of hinted at marriage a few times lately, just to see her reactions. Can't say that she jumped for joy, but I guess I couldn't expect a teen age reaction. She never said no. Of course, come to think of it, I never came out and really asked her if she would marry me. I was just sort of talking about how nice it would be if we could really be together all of the time - I remember I thought that her reply was rather wishy-washy. She just smiled and said, "All in good time". What had I expected? She probably thought I just wanted her to move in with me and live the good life but without me making any sort of commitment to her. I think I'd better get myself thinking more clearly and making my feelings clear to her. *Soon, Bill, Soon.*

I was watching TV - think it was about 5:30 when the doorbell rang. I really jumped that time. It was the police. Finally, Ella had been found. I knew that they would somehow notify me, being as I seemed to be the only remaining "relative" that Ella had. I knew that she had listed me as the person to notify in case of any emergency. When they came in and told me what happened, I put on quite a show.

First, I sort of reeled in disbelief, and then with a quivering voice *(that wasn't all completely an act, I must say).* I asked them "Who did it? And why?" They answered that they didn't have any answers as yet, and that at this point they were still investigating

They did say that it seemed to be a robbery that had been taking place when she must have come home and interrupted. Good - just as I had planned!!! Still, with my voice quivering, I told them how dear she was to me and went on about all of the wonderful times we had shared when I had gone over there for dinners, etc. (That should cover it as they would probably find some of my fingerprints around her place in many various locations.) I think I went on asking them "When did this happen?" They said they weren't sure at this time. I went on "How did you find out about it?" They went on to relate that the Becker's had called them. They stated that they had been trying to call her and even went down and knocked very loudly on her door and there was no response - that's when they called 911. They went on to say, "The Becker's had stated that you were probably the person who should be notified, and that you had called them with some concerns because you hadn't been able to contact her". They then asked if they could ask a few questions, and I told that them I would be more than willing if anything might help find who had killed her.

Chapter 19

THE INTERROGATION

There were two officers who came to the door, as is I suppose, the correct protocol. At any rate, I suggested that we sit at the kitchen table - always heard that things seemed friendlier around the table. I even asked them if I could make them a pot of coffee, which they declined. Oh well, that was fine, I could possibly have seemed a bit shaky drinking coffee, whereas I could either fold my hands together or place them firmly on the table if we were just talking.

They started out the conversation just asking about my relationship with Ella. I then went back into a lot of history - telling them that I had worked for her husband Mac at Conner's Computer firm, so that I had known her for many, many years. I repeated so much of the history - about meeting Rosie and being married, but still working there, even after we were divorced. I made special note of the fact that Ella and I remained on very good terms even after that, and then, after Rosie died, she had asked me to remain in the company, and our relationship had always remained very good. I emphasized the fact that I sort of tried to help her whenever I could and took care of any small chores in the condo whenever there was something to do. They of course interjected some questions along the way, and one of them seemed to be making a few notations on the note pad he had in front of him. I even went into telling them of how many times I would join Ella for dinner and what a good cook she was. Figured I'd take this opportunity to put emphasis on the fact that I was over there a lot so there wouldn't be any suspicions when they found my fingerprints in most of the areas of Ella's condo.

After all of that they seemed quite well satisfied, but then they asked a few more questions about what I had been doing over the weekend. I was caught a little off guard, which I suppose was good. I blurted out "What? are you thinking that I may have something to do with it?" Probably not the best response, but they smiled and one of them - think his name was Dick said, "These are just questions that we have to ask - please don't take any offense." I apologized for raising my voice, and went on to relay all that I had done - eating out, purchasing the dress, etc. I told them that I had receipts, and that there were people there who they could talk to if they had any doubts. That seemed to open up some more questions - was this dress for Ella?, Could you tell us who it was for? When I explained that it was for Lola, the questions went into another direction, so I explained about Lola and that she also was a friend of Ella's and was a visitor over at the condo on several occasions. This brought up a thought that had never entered my mind before - Lola's fingerprints would probably be found also - thank heavens, now I had explained them away, seemingly to their satisfaction. Then they said, "We'd appreciate it if you wouldn't leave town or anything". I replied that I certainly had no intentions of leaving town.

Then I thought about some more questions that I should ask them. "What did you do with Ella's body? Where is she?" They explained that the coroner had been called and the body was at the city morgue. I got a little overwhelmed by all of this news, guess I hadn't thought about the next stages. They went on to say "When we get the final results about everything, we'll notify you - I suppose that you'll want to make funeral arrangements, etc." I stumbled a bit when I replied "Yes, yes of course - there probably will be lots of things to be taken care of." Then Dick continued "In the meantime, the condo is being held as a crime scene, so we'd appreciate it if you do not come over there. We'll let you know when you can be there, but it may be a while." "Thank you for your time and your cooperation - we will be in touch and keep you informed". "How did you find me?" I finally inquired. They explained that they had questioned everyone in the building, and several knew of me, but then it was the Becker's that had given them my address and phone number.

That sort of shocked me - guess I hadn't gotten that far in the thinking process. I was extremely relieved when they left, and I sat in the recliner, closed my eyes and just let everything sink in. Where do we go from here? Funeral arrangements, contacting Conner's, contacting friends, her church, this was by no means over, it was simply just moving on to more problems, commitments, putting on good fronts for so many more people and for so many more occasions. I was overwhelmed. *Yeah Mom, I hear you again with your old warning - "Oh what a tangled web we weave, when once we practice to deceive!" You did it, Bill, you're in it up to your neck - better be careful or it may start getting higher and smother you.* I needed some comfort, some help. I called Lola to see if she was home yet.

Chapter 20

MAYBE LOLA CAN HELP ME

The phone was on the forth ring - the final one before her message machine went on, and I was almost getting weepy, but thank God, she picked up and I heard that beautiful, wonderful voice say "Hello, it's Lola". Just those three words were somehow a bit comforting to me. As I started to speak, I found my voice was still shaky, but I somehow managed to tell her what had happened. I guess I must have sounded so upset, that even though it was almost 8:00, she said that she would be right over. I was so relieved and thankful - if she can just help me make it through another night. I didn't know if I should mix up a drink or make a pot of coffee, but rather than decide, did both. I started to sip on my drink while the coffee was brewing. I could have belted down a couple very quickly, but still being careful to restrain myself, just took slow sips, and I think it helped me to pull myself together.

When she arrived, she came to me and put her arms around me, kissed me - first gently on the forehead, and then quite passionately on the lips. At this I reveled, reminding myself that this was just how I wanted everything to turn out. I gratefully hugged her and thanked her for coming over.

After I got a cup of coffee for her and we sat down, I started almost babbling - having to explode without having to watch every word - just to share everything with her and know that she wouldn't try to question me on everything. It felt so good. She asked me if I had had anything to eat, and I realized that I hadn't had anything since that piece of toast in the morning. She then searched the refrigerator and found some lunch meat and made me a sandwich. It wasn't until then that I realized I felt the twinges of hunger and knew that I needed it. She also made half of a one for herself. She refreshed her coffee and I had a cup also.

Now it was her turn to ask some questions. I had told her about all of the police matters, but she was thinking ahead. She then asked about funeral arrangements. I told her that the police had to release both the body and entrance to the condo wouldn't be possible until after they had finalized their investigations, and who knows when that would be. "Regardless," she said, "We still have to think about a lot of details. We'll have to contact the church, probably look in her address book and notify friends, think about funeral arrangements, etc." I nodded at all of these suggestions, agreeing with her on everything. I then said, "Of course the biggest task I will have immediately is to contact Conner's and let them know what has happened". I guess Lola hadn't even thought about that. "Oh honey, that definitely should be the first step." I continued "Think I'll just contact the CEO and ask him to set up a board meeting - then I can announce to everyone what has happened. I know it won't make any difference in the running of the company, but I think it would be good to have them hear the news from me instead of reading it as headlines in the newspaper". "Good thinking ", she responded. "You'd better get that call in first thing in the morning." I nodded my head. I knew that they usually had board meetings on Mondays, so it shouldn't be too hard to have the secretary round them up for, well maybe 10:30 would be good. Some of the people were still working there, but there were some of them, like me, who had retired, so hopefully they would be available.

Lola then started asking more about funeral arrangements. I hadn't covered that in my thoughts as yet, but I suppose it would have to be thought on. I would have just suggested cremation, but Ella had discussed that with many of her friends in the last couple of years, and she took quite a stand against that. She wanted the full services, just as she had had for Mac and as she had insisted upon for Rosie. I had to have things as I knew she would have wanted, but I expressed to Lola that I was not going to have a reviewal the night before. She was a little taken aback at that, but I said I didn't want to have to go through that. I did relent a little and suggested a reviewal one hour before the service. I supposed that could at least be done that way, standing by old traditional ways, but making things as easy for me as possible.

I told her that I really didn't want to talk about things anymore - and we would have to wait until the police gave us the go ahead anyhow. She only asked one thing, and that was that I should call the minister of Ella's church and at least inform him as to what was going one, "OK", I said, "I promise to do that tomorrow morning right after I make the phone call to Conner's - now could you just hold me for a little while?" She smiled and led me back into the living room.

She took the aggressive position this time, with her arms around me - rubbing my shoulders a bit, giving light kisses and whispering in my ear about how much she loved me, and how she knew that I would take care of everything. She kept assuring me that I had been such a good friend to Ella and how she admired so much all that I was always doing for her and helping to make her life as good and as comfortable as I could. It almost made me feel a bit guilty, but as her soft body stayed so close to me, my feelings of guilt passed over, and the thought of a lifetime ahead with Lola just kept creeping more and more. I know it may not have been an appropriate time, but I started getting aroused and couldn't help myself but show Lola how much I wanted her. She maybe didn't think it was the appropriate time either, but somehow, I think she just wanted to do anything that may make me feel better, and she sure knew how to do that. I finally whispered into her ear "Darling, would you please stay with me tonight? I really need you and want you". She barely whispered "OK" and walked with me into the bedroom.

This was a new role for her - she was sort of, well, in a way mothering me. She tenderly undressed me, tucking me under the covers as she undressed and then slid in next to me. My body was just getting warm under the blankets, and when her cool flesh moved in next to me, it was like an invitation to cuddle her and make her feel toasty also, which I did. I just held her for a while, rocking gently back and forth and she seemed to enjoy it, but soon I found that I had to put my head between her breasts, and she pressed it close to her, and another sexual encounter began.

She seemed even more gentle and tender than she ever had before. At this point I didn't even care of I had an orgasm or not - I was just being loved and adored, and perhaps she felt the same way, as it was just comforting, and that seemed to be all that she really wanted to do, was to comfort me. I felt her, touched her, but didn't really try to arouse her - just sighed in contentment and finally, with my arms circling around her, I fell asleep. Cradled in warmth and love, just what I really needed tonight.

$$—\ \textit{Q}\!\!\swarrow\ —$$

Chapter 21

IMPORTANT THINGS
TO TEND TO.

We both got up early the next morning. I showered and got somewhat dressed up. I had been enjoying not having to put on a suit, shirt and tie every morning. I debated if I should because of the board meeting, but opted to put on a shirt and tie, but just a sweater vest - a sort of in-between outfit. I asked Lola if she thought it was OK, and she said she thought I looked just fine. That was indeed good enough for me. I did put my arms around her and thanked her for being there for me over night. I told her that having her with me was so nice, and really helped me during a bad time. Funny in a way, I wondered momentarily if she would have been quite so comforting if she knew the real story. *Don't start that - too many things that have to be kept clear in my head. I was sure that there would be many questions coming up from everyone, and I'd better get the story straight in my head and not goof up on anything.*

I made the call to Conner's right after 8:00. Henry was extremely shocked when I related what had happened. He also agreed with me that it was a good idea to call a board meeting as soon as possible. After looking at his schedule, he suggested 10:30, and said he would have his secretary call everyone right away. There, that was done.

I then sat and had another cup of coffee with Lola. She said that she had a few things to catch up on at home because of being gone for a few days and asked if I'd be OK without her going with me. I assured that I would be all right. She then suggested that she would bring something over for dinner and eat with me. I smiled and told her that she was so kind and helpful, and added that it just made me love her even more.

She kissed me lightly, tousled my hair a bit - she knows that always bugs me and I just feel compelled to immediately get it straightened and combed, which made her chuckle.

Yes, it bugged me, but I really found it sort of special - just something between the two of us, and that was nice. She then gave me another kiss, got her coat on and turned as she was leaving and blew a sweet kiss my way. Wow, she was really something.

When I got to Conner's, about 10:00, Henry's secretary informed me that all but 1 of the board members were able to come. She said that everyone was really curious as to what was going on, but she said that she hadn't given any hints - felt it was better that everyone found out at the same time, and not have rumors straggling about. Jean was a smart cookie - that's obviously why she was an Executive Secretary. I knew that Henry had made a wise choice when he chose her, and she had proved invaluable to him on more than one occasion. I had time enough to walk through a couple of departments and saw a few people who were still there whom I had known years ago. I said "Hi, how are you doing", but didn't linger long enough to start any conversations. Some of them nodded their heads up and down, which I thought was a little odd, but then just got on with the business of the day. I told them that I was there for a board meeting and had a little time to spare, so was just doing a walkthrough of familiar territories. They really had a pretty good crew working there. Thinking back on my years there in the finance department, I believe I could only remember 3 persons who had to be let go - that was a pretty good record for a good size company like this. Naturally there were turn overs, but also a lot of people who had been there for several years and seemed to be content with their lots. Pretty good for any company this day of age.

Finally, it was time - I filed into the conference room and took what seemed to be my usual seat. I smiled and just made a little chit-chat until Henry walked in, sat down, and informed them all that "We have something very serious, and most shocking to tell all of you this morning" in case you don't know. I thought that was a strange comment but didn't interrupt.   He then went on to make the announcement about Ella's murder. I wasn't sure just how he was going to handle the situation, if he would tell them or direct it then to me. I was indeed thankful that he had stepped up to the duty. Then he asked if there were questions and suggested that perhaps I may be able to answer them.

Now it was my turn. There were several questions from most all of them, but of course I had a pretty pat answer - that the police were still investigating and that they would keep me informed when they had any concrete answers. Then finally the conversations sort of went back into reminiscing and sharing stories about Ella and Mac. At that point I think I felt that I had done an OK job and gotten over a big hurdle. A couple of them did ask about funeral arrangements, etc., but I had to give them the same answer, that the timing of that would depend upon the police investigation. Some asked about suggestions for memorials. I brilliantly suggested that probably Ella would be happiest if they would contribute to the scholarship fund that she had started in memory of Rosie, or else any of their favorite memorials. They seemed to think that made sense and agreed that it would indeed be a good tribute to Rosie, Mac and Ella.

I was beginning to feel very confident that all seemed to be going as well as could be expected. When I was on my way back to my place, I stopped in the store, just picked up some bread and butter which I knew I needed, but then walked by the floral department and spotted a nice bouquet - nothing elegant, just pretty and decided to get it for the middle of the table when Lola came over tonight.

When I got home, I suddenly remembered that I'd forgotten to call the church. Oh oh, better get that taken care of. Lola certainly would be disappointed with me if I'd forgotten that detail. Oh dear - oh of course, almost forgot the name of the minister. The name of the church was simple enough. First Lutheran. *Think a minute - Borg? Berg? Oh come on Bill, think hard.   ------Oberg - yep, that was it. Pastor Robert Oberg.* I didn't have the number written down but didn't have to look it up. I remembered Ella telling me that it was one of the best numbers a church could have, 587-8463, but reading Just God. Guess it is true, when you hear something unusual like that, it sticks in your mind. Well, here goes - another hurdle to get over.

"Hello, wondering if Pastor Oberg might be available - this is Bill Anderson, a friend of Ella Conner. Yes, I'll hold a moment OK, thanks. "Hi Pastor Oberg" Again I explained who I was and went on "-I'm afraid I have some distressing news to tell you." I then went on to relate all that had happened. He was indeed upset to hear it. He too asked about funeral arrangements, and once again I reported that the police were still investigating and would keep me advised. I did suggest that perhaps it wouldn't quite be appropriate at this time to tell anyone else any of the details - just that Ella was dead. He agreed with me, and thanked me for getting in touch with him, and that he'd be willing to meet with me at any time to discuss funeral arrangements. Suddenly funeral arrangements seemed to be high on everyone's agenda.

Well, I guess it should be high on my agenda also, after all when we got the go ahead from the police for taking care of the funeral, I could probably breathe a little easier - knowing that they hadn't come up with any pertinent evidence as to who murdered Ella. *I smiled as I thought back on a game we used to play when we were kids - "I know something you don't know". Silly, but it just popped into my mind.*

Now I thought I'd just pick up the house a little - do some dishes, so it would look better when Lola arrived. I wasn't just exactly sure when that might be, but likely towards 5:00 so we could have a drink, or wine or something and have a little cocktail hour before dinner. That really sounded most appealing to me. I turned on some nice CD's and just took my time getting ready for another special evening. I was beginning to think now of the future. I knew this wasn't exactly the right time to ask Lola to marry me, but I had made up my mind that I really wanted her as my wife. Just think, when I got all of the money, we'd be living on easy street for the rest of our lives. Funny, but suddenly thoughts of being wealthy were becoming high on my list of wants and needs. I had never had such desires before, and had been most content, feeling that I had more than enough. Certainly, while growing up I never even thought of wealth - just of hopefully making ends meet. I do remember times when I was a teenager that there were times when money was tough to come by. Poor Dad, he always worked so hard, but didn't have anything to spare. I know he was glad that he could at least take good care of all of us and we certainly never suffered. *What was that song that he'd sing to Mom at that time? "Oh Yeah - I Can't Give You Anything but Love, Baby" and then he'd twirl her around, take her in his arms and kiss her. Seems it always would work - she would smile, her eyes would twinkle, and they were like teenagers themselves.* Oh, those old memories were always so pleasant, and so comforting to me, but I didn't dare slide back too much. I could never have imagined then that someday I would never have to worry about money and would be able to do anything that I wanted to do. I almost felt giddy, and my imagination started whirling about the opportunities that may arise and what I'd really want when I knew I'd actually be able to have it.

Chapter 22

NOW TIME FOR PLEASANT DREAMS

I stretched out on the sofa, closed my eyes and just started day dreaming. The first thing that came up in my vision was Lola and I as one. When I thought of marrying her and going on a Honeymoon, I had decided on Jamaica, but while I was thinking of that, I got a bit diverted - I thought about the condo in Grand Cayman. Guess what? It would probably be possible for me to possess that, of course it would be a part of the inheritance package and may have to go through probate – I wasn't sure how she had all of that arranged for, or if indeed she did have it all arranged. Oh well, I probably could manage somehow to have first bid on it. Wouldn't it be something though to have a place in Grand Cayman? That was indeed a piece of heaven on earth.

Better not get ahead of yourself old boy. Just concentrate on how things will go for the next week or so, but the dreams continued. Oh Dad, I can really, honestly hear you singing so clearly lately - what would you sing for me now? Bet I've got it - think you said Ethel Merman sang this in the Play Gypsy the words were "Everything's Coming Up Roses for You and For Me" yes, Lola, I think that will be our theme song from here on in. Thanks Dad, you always found the right song to describe every situation - that might be fun, now instead of just hearing you, I may just join right in with you.

I got back into my day dreaming mode, even started dreaming

about hiring a private jet to take Lola and I down to the Condo. Who knows, maybe while we are down there, we'd fly over and check out Cayman Brac and Little Cayman. I know that Rosie and her folks had been over to Cayman Brac one time. They had talked about an experience one evening while there that is a phenomenon sometimes on those islands - they saw "The Green Flash." Conditions have to be just right at sunset time, with no clouds in the sky, etc. At any rate, just as the sun seems to drown into the ocean, there is a second when this green flash appears. Many have seen it, but it's pretty rare. Of the many times they had been down there, that was the only time that they had seen it. Guess it's something like the Blue Moon - there really is such a thing, but it doesn't happen too often. Maybe some evening Lola and I would be able to witness it. Rosie had told me that the Scuba diving was even more spectacular on The Brac than it was on the big island. She also said the beaches were lovely, but that the island also had some huge bluffs with caves in them that were awesome.

Yes, Lola and I could check it all out, and then just jet over to see Little Cayman also. That was still supposed to be lightly inhabited and more primitive than the other sister islands. The thoughts kept on building and I was getting excited about all of them. *Slow down - OK Daddy, I know what you'd be singing now "Money Is the Root of All Evil".* Maybe back then I could have convinced myself that the saying was true, but now I merely saw it as an opportunity building up, and the joys would be awesome. I was sure that I could handle it all - I wouldn't let it go to my head.

I had fallen in love with Cayman when Rosie and I spent our honeymoon there, and we'd been fortunate enough to go back and visit 3 more times before she died. Not for 2 weeks, but enough time to renew ourselves during the winter and take a little sunshine break. Amazing what a few days of sunshine can do for one's souls when it's cold and there's snow on the ground. Maybe that's why it even seemed more like a little heaven on earth, because of the season change.

Well, maybe Jamaica will be another wonderful adventure - at least I knew that if Lola was with me, she would make it another heavenly spot.

In my mind I thought about that travel channel special I had seen. - Everything from a Rain Forest to Falls that you could climb up from the bottom and walk through. The legend of Rose Hall - Tulip Trees, Errol Flynn's Island - Banana's, Pineapple, Mango's. What fun we'd have. I knew that I wouldn't be able to wait too much longer before I asked Lola to marry me, but I also knew that I had to let this whole episode about Ella pass over first. I wonder how the police are doing - if they in fact have found anything new? I was feeling tempted to call them but figured that I'd better let some time elapse - my only excuse would be that I was wondering about making funeral arrangements, and they had told me that they would be in touch and keep me informed as to when I would be able to do that. It was beginning to gnaw at me just a little though - which would seem more suspicious? To keep at them or just bide my time and wait for them to make the move. *Gosh - it's almost 5:00 - I'd better just clear my mind and be ready for cocktail time.*

I went out to the kitchen - remembered that there were a few crackers left, and I was pretty sure that there was some cheese also, so I set about making a little plate of cheese and crackers, just so Lola would know that I was looking forward to her joining me - and that I certainly was. There's the doorbell – I had finished just in time. I rushed to answer it, and there was my beautiful wife to be - hope she'd see it that way too.

Lola had a couple of bags with her, so I helped her with them and carried them out into the kitchen while she took her coat off. I hadn't been sure if she would be bringing a selection from a deli, Chinese or whatever route she may have desired. I was delighted to see that she had just brought preparations for cooking something for us. She had 2 beautiful thick cut pork chops, some fresh broccoli, 2 sweet potatoes and a couple of bread sticks. Wow, it looked like it was going to be a great meal. She even had a couple of apple turnovers for dessert. Yep, this gal took care of everything. Easy to see why I loved her so much - beautiful, gentle, loving and a good cook to boot. I told her that we didn't have to eat right away, so suggested that perhaps we could have a drink - showing her that I had the plate of cheese and crackers all ready. I then also said that I'd be happy to help her make dinner after. She didn't really need much persuasion, so we put the meat in the refrigerator and went back to sit in the living room. I asked her if she'd like me to build a little fire in the fireplace for her, and she nodded and said that would really be very nice, so that was my next project. It didn't really take very long, I always liked to have all of the makings for a fire handy - some paper, kindling or sometimes even some pine cones to get it going and an assortment of logs that were nice and dry and caught fire easily. Also tried to have enough to keep the fire going for a while - *yes Dad, I hear you, "Throw Another Log On The Fire" - I've got to stop doing that, it seems more and more like I really hear his voice - almost as if he was still here just standing by me.*

Lola was seated on the sofa, so that looked like the best spot to sit down and be close to her. I put the cheese on the cocktail table in front of the sofa and asked her what she wanted to drink. I knew she liked a couple of different cocktails, but many times she just preferred white wine, and that's what she requested now.

I just started the conversation by asking her first what she had done during the day. She told me that she had called some of her friends and told them about what happened to Ella. I was surprised, and she realized it and said, "Didn't you read this morning's paper?" I admitted that I had brought it in, but with the board meeting and all I didn't even look at it. "Well, perhaps you'd better do that now". I obliged and got the paper and opened it up, and there it was. Not exactly the headline, thankfully, but it did make an article on the front page. I sort of scanned the article - not reading everything word for word, but it did tell that a well- known, former owner of Conner's Computer company had been discovered murdered in her condo. Now I understood why some of the employees there had sort of nodded when I said we were having a board meeting. I also got the meaning of when Henry had said. " In case you don't know as yet" The article stated that the police were continuing their investigation, but at this point they had as yet not found the murderer.

I could feel Lola watching me as I read it. "Well," I said, "I guess

I'm glad that it's finally all made public, probably best that way." Lola nodded, and continued on, listing some of the people she had contacted. I guess she was surprised that I hadn't had any calls from anyone. I didn't want to admit that I hadn't even checked the message machine when I got home, and she didn't press it any further, so I just made a mental note to myself that perhaps I'd better check it later. After she finished with her news, she asked me about the board meeting. I told her that all went pretty well. I guess I had been a bit surprised that some of the people hadn't seemed too shocked - stupid me! Most of them had probably seen the newspaper, so were not surprised to have the emergency meeting. Oh well, I did my duty. I related all about the conversations as well as I could remember. I never had been very good at passing on information - Rosie had told me that a million times - "Whenever I ask how things went you just say fine - period. I want to know all of the details". Not necessary as far as I was concerned, guess it must just be a female thing that they want blow by blow descriptions and clear accounts of everything.

I did say that they had asked about the funeral, etc. and that I had suggested that they set up memorials to be designated for the Scholarship fund in Rosie's memory. She thought that was a good suggestion and commended me for voicing it to them. Then she brought up the subject of the funeral also. "I suppose that you should meet with Pastor Oberg and at least outline a few things that you may want, or that you may know that Ella had wanted." "If you would like me to, I'd be happy to go with you when you speak to him, or would that be awkward for you?" I thanked her and said, "that would be wonderful I'm sure that he knows you knew Ella and Rosie and also Ella told me once that she had told Pastor Oberg that you and I were enjoying one another's company, and that it pleased her very much and that she was happy about our relationship." That seemed to please any anxieties she may have had, as she smiled and said "OK, that's good to know. Just let me know when you make an appointment with him."

By this time, she figured it was time she got out into the kitchen and start dinner. I agreed but went out there with her so that we could continue talking. She commented on the flowers and said that it was very nice of me to think of doing such a sweet thing. *Chalk up another good deed, Bill - I knew she really liked flowers.* I asked her if there was anything that I could do to help her, and she said that if I wanted to set the table, that would be nice. We just continued with a little chit-chat while I was doing that. I did my best to put everything where it should be - between Mom and Susie, they made sure that all of us boys at least learned the proper way to do things. Not that we did it that way when it was our turn to set the table - everyone in the family was grateful just to have all the utensils they needed - regardless of which side of the plate it may be sitting on. Afraid we were spoiled by having Mom and Susie in the family. We guys always figured that was women's work and didn't know why we had to bother to learn any of that sort of stuff. As I was doing this, it suddenly donned upon me that I might even be glad they had harped on me - I could now impress Lola that I had been brought up properly and could do even things like setting a table in the proper way - fork on the left of the plate, knife on the right, with the blade side of the knife turned towards the plate, then the spoon next to it. If there was a salad fork on the table, that was placed on the left of the fork, so it was in the right order to use when you ate - salad fork first, then dinner fork. *I was pretty sure that Mom was watching and would be proud of me, silly thoughts, perhaps, but thoughts that once again pulled me back to my growing up years. They were indeed good.* The meal was starting to smell darn good by now, and I was really looking forward to it, both because I was hungry, and because I would be sitting looking at my beautiful Lola while we were eating.

When we were done, I helped clear the table, and then I went back into the living room and stirred up the fire and added some more logs. By the time I got back to the kitchen, she had dessert and coffee ready to be enjoyed. The turnovers were very good, and I told her that everything had been wonderful and thanked her for being so nice and coming over to make me a meal. I was this close to proposing to her right then and there, but somehow didn't think that this would be quite the appropriate time. I did make the decision however that this was going to be the right evening to give her the beautiful blue dress which was hiding on the top shelf in my closet. I just couldn't keep the surprise buried any longer - I just wanted so much to see how she would like it and then to ask her to please put it on for me, adding to myself that I'd gladly help her take it off again. *Contain yourself, Bill - you'll have a lifetime to quench your desires, but right now all I could think about was this evening.*

Chapter23

I HOPE THE TIMING
WILL BE RIGHT

I finally suggested that it would be nice to have another cup of coffee out by the fire and just enjoy it, and she agreed. I carried both of our cups out there and put them on the cocktail table, and she brought out the coffee pot and filled them both. This was a special time, and I didn't want to open my mind to any thoughts about the outside world, this was just our time, and sitting right here was for the moment our world, and it was a most pleasant world. After a few minutes, I told her that I had a surprise for her. I got up and went into the bedroom and came out with the dress, all wrapped so beautifully, and handed it to her. She looked up at me and said "Bill, what in the world is it?" I just smiled and told her to open it up. She continued though "Why do I get a present?

It's not my birthday or anything - this is too much". Yet, I could see her eyes smiling in anticipation and she started removing the ribbons and the beautiful bow. Her hands almost seemed to tremble a bit when she finally had the ribbons pulled away from the box and began to open the it. There was still a little more to go by the time she pulled back the many pieces of tissue paper and saw the beautiful blue dress. Her eyes were sort of misty when she gasped and said, "Oh Bill, it's just gorgeous, but I can't understand why you picked it out." She did however stand up and hold the dress in front of her - oh man was that going to look spectacular on her. "When did you go shopping?" she asked. I then explained that I missed her so much when she was gone that when I had gone out to eat, I saw this in the window at Wrights and really wanted her to have it because I thought she'd look so beautiful in it. She smiled broadly as she thanked me most profusely, including a hug and a kiss. I asked her if she would mind trying it on for me so I could make sure that it fit her. She gladly accepted saying that she wanted to be able to look in the mirror anyhow and see how it looked. I smiled to myself as she closed the bedroom door behind her when she went in to change - as if I hadn't seen her from top to bottom before, oh well, guess it's nice to have her act sort of shy anyhow.

Within a couple of minutes, she opened the door and walked out, and it was like a vision appearing oh did she look gorgeous. I couldn't help it - I found myself singing *"Oh, You Beautiful Doll"*. She looked at me with a startled expression on her face, I couldn't blame her, I was startled too - it had just suddenly popped out of my mouth. I was embarrassed, but I went on to explain that my Dad used to sing old songs that would seem to fit various occasions, and when I saw her that song just came into my mind and I just had to sing it. Then she smiled and said, "That's pretty cool, so thank you." "The dress is so pretty, and it fits perfectly, - how in the world did you know what size and everything?" I quickly came back with "well, I always heard that size 12 was the perfect size, and of course you're perfect, so I just knew it would fit." She smiled again and once again gave me a hug and a kiss. I was so tempted to ask her right then and there if she would marry me but wasn't sure if this was the right time or not. Instead I thought I'd sort of feel her out. When she said she was going back to change, I asked her if she'd like some help and told her I'd be more than willing to do so. She looked a little pensive for a moment, but then smiled and said, "I think I'd like that very much". That's all I needed to hear - to me, the invitation had been issued.

I did follow her into the bedroom, and very gently undid the back buttons at the neckline as she undid the belt. The soft supple material of the long sleeves hung so beautifully on those lovely arms as she undid the two small buttons on the wrists.

I gently then helped her lift the dress over her head, thinking that I was unwrapping the most gorgeous gift that there was - Lola. I would have happily rejoiced in just completing the unwrapping as that moment, but she insisted that she wanted to carefully put it on a hanger in the closet before doing anything else. Thank heavens that only took a couple of minutes so I could go back and continue unwrapping her beautiful body. She then, as she had done before, began helping me to undress. By the time she finished, with some well-placed caresses along the way, I was ready for anything. I pulled back the covers on the bed and I laid down close to her and proceeded to entwine her in my arms and feel those lovely, and by this time familiar curves. My God she was so wonderful - I could have hugged her with all my strength but restrained myself so that I wouldn't take her breath away. She was a fragile doll, and I wanted to play with her as long as possible. I loved this part of all of the foreplay - exploring her with my finger tips and my lips, oh she tasted so delicious and smelled like an exotic flower. She had this wonderful way of wriggling around in bed so that her body touched each part of my body in just the right way, making us feel like we were one before we actually became one. It was good. I was pretty good at holding off until I knew she was finding it hard to wait, but tonight I just needed release - I finally knew I couldn't wait much longer and whispered, "Are you ready?" She whispered OK and opened her legs to let me in. I didn't want to hurt her and disciplined myself to go in just a little bit before I just had to get in as far as possible and came with a frenzy that I hadn't felt since my wild times with Rosie. Luckily, she seemed to get worked up quite rapidly also, knowing that I was ready to come, and I think she came also. I'm not sure - I've heard that sometimes women sort of pretend that they have had an orgasm just to make the male feel like he had succeeded in pleasing her, but if that was the case, she was doing a dam good job of acting. Yes, I think she really did come.

When I finally rolled over and held her in my arms, I couldn't stand it anymore. I kissed her and said "Darling, I love you so much - this may not be the right time, but I want you and need you so - I want to spend the rest of my life with you - Lola, will you marry me?"   She didn't say anything at first, and I thought. *Oh God, Bill, you blew it - this isn't the way I wanted to propose - she'll think I'm just an animal who lives for sex.* I said, "Oh honey, I wanted this to be at just the right time, and maybe it wasn't, I'm sorry".   She then put her arms around me and said "Don't apologize - no matter when it might have come, I've wanted it to happen, and this is a perfect time. Yes, Bill, I would love to be your wife." I could hardly believe that she had really accepted, and that I had had guts enough to pop the question - in bed of all things.

Well, you did it and she accepted. She didn't even talk about leaving that night, we just enjoyed one another's bodies and I fell asleep dreaming of being able to be in bed with her every night and every day for the rest of my life. Yep Daddy, "I'm in Heaven, Yes in Heaven". That's the right song. And then I was sleeping.

Chapter 24

WAS IT A DREAM?

When I woke up in the morning, Lola was still in bed, but she wasn't sleeping either.

I looked at her and smiled and said "I'm afraid to ask for fear it may have been just one wonderful dream. Did you really say that you will be my wife?" She laughed and said, "Well, if it was a dream, I seem to have had the exact same dream, and my answer was yes then, and it's still yes now." I put my arms around her and kissed her and told her how happy I was and that I planned on making our life together as wonderful as possible.

Then she got up to take a shower and get dressed. I just laid in bed thinking about oh so many things - high on the list of course was that Lola had actually accepted my proposal. That was good, but the timing wasn't good at all - we'd have to walk very slowly until we were sure it was the right time to announce it to everyone. I figured that I'd better talk to her seriously while we were having coffee and some breakfast. By then she was showered and dressed and said she'd make some coffee while I got ready, so that was the first plan.

When I got out to the kitchen I could hardly wait for some coffee - it smelled wonderful. She poured some juice and put some bread in the toaster while she got the butter and jam on the table. I then told her that we'd better talk some more about our personal plans and suggested that no matter how much I would love to announce to the world that we were going to get married, I thought it better to wait a couple of weeks until Ella's funeral was over. There would be so many things to take care of right now, and I wanted to be able to give my full attention to her when we could go pick out a ring, and maybe even have an engagement party to let our friends in on our plans. I wasn't sure how she was going to take all of that, but surprisingly enough, she seemed agreeable to those ideas. I guess she probably knew that it would be better, and said "You're right, Bill, we have to make first plans first, and the rest will follow in good time. I'll not change my mind though, so don't think you can wriggle out of it later" she giggled as she tussled my hair and tickled me at the same time. Playful little creature - she'd often just catch me off guard with some silliness, and it delighted me.

After I had some toast, I started asking her what she thought about funeral arrangements. She'd talked about them right away after hearing about Ella's death, but I hadn't really made any plans, and at this point even I thought it was time to get some things squared away. That opened the subject up, and she walked over to the little desk in the corner and got some paper and a pencil. She suggested that we write down some things so that when we met with Pastor Oberg, he'd know that we had put some thought into what Ella wanted and would like. Now, she took over and that was fine. She knew what Ella liked, and she of course had been there for both Mac and Rosie's funeral, and they were quite similar, so she figured that the same format should be used again. She was sure that Pastor Oberg would also have suggestions about music, organist, soloist if we wanted any, etc. I knew that I wouldn't be much help along those lines, so as far as I was concerned, anything that he might suggest would fit in just fine. When Lola seemed satisfied that she had everything written down that she felt was necessary she seemed pleased that we had taken those steps. I did give her a suggestion and an opinion about flowers. I felt that I should have two large matching bouquets on either side of the casket. Oh, that opened up a new subject, we'd have to decide what funeral director was going to handle the funeral, and pick out a casket. That was fundamental, but I hadn't even given it a thought up to now. Good thing that Lola was making me think about these things, I guess. I thought back on Rosie's funeral and remembered that the funeral home was called Winstead's. As soon as I got the go ahead from the police, I said I'd give them a call. In fact, I told Lola that if I hadn't been contacted by the police by this afternoon, I'd call and see what was going on. They certainly couldn't hold the body at the morgue forever. Who knows, maybe it would be a good move - they may think it strange if I don't even care enough to call and find out what is going on. That's the plan for today.

Lola then surprised me by saying that she really didn't have anything special to do today, so if I wanted her to stay around just for some company and to see if we could take care of any more details, she'd be glad to spend the day with me. An offer I certainly couldn't refuse. She also said that she thought I should call the police, after all it had been 3 days that had passed now, and they'd certainly know that funeral arrangements had to be made. Well, I told her that I would wait until after lunch - then if I hadn't heard I would call and at least try to get somewhat of a definite answer. I also had thought of some other things that I needed to find answers for - Ella's personal records - how to get her lawyers name, any pertinent records to be found - there would be bills to take care of, final details to handle - closing accounts, etc. Suddenly there seemed to be a million little things that I realized that it was just me who had to deal with everything, and the idea of that was beginning to loom very large ahead of me. I felt a little squeamish. *Hang on, Bill, this is no time to start losing it - this was getting close to the finish line - close to happily ever after - close to the beginning of a new life to me. I only had to go a little further, take a few deep breaths - slow yourself down.* Lola noticed my actions and patted me on the shoulders saying "You'll be OK, honey, I'm sure that you will take care of everything in just the right way. I decided that I'd better make some lists also so that I'd at least be able to find out the financial situation. I figured that I'd probably be stuck with some of the bills for a while, or at least find out how they took care of such situations and how some money could be accessed to take care of some of the things. Afraid I needed to find out some things and keep up on what needed to be done.

Next step was to pick up phone messages, I found that both of my brothers and Susie also had called to express their shock about hearing about Ella and each of them asked me to give them a call with details. That was nice of them to make contact anyhow - we always were close. I'll tell them that Dad had been taking care of ----------*what are you saying Bill?   Dad hasn't been here, or was he?* I'd been starting to doubt some of my thoughts lately - no time for this - I don't want to start having strange thoughts again.

Can't do this - concentrate.

I then looked up the number for the funeral director, and at least got that written on the paper - then one with Pastor Oberg's name and number on it. Yes, I wanted to be all prepared, so when the time was right, we can get everything organized at the same time.

Part 3

Chapter 25

AN OK TO MAKE ARRANGEMENTS.

It was just about 1:00 PM, and the phone rang, finally it was the police. First on the agenda was the fact that in their searching, they were not able to locate any closer relatives, so it seemed that I was the logical one to handle everything. Duh!!! That much I knew, and I was sure that I already had told them that. They then went on to say that I could select a funeral director who could pick up Ella's body at the city morgue and I could go ahead with funeral arrangements. They said that the funeral directors should know the procedure of how that all worked, and if not, the people at the morgue would explain about everything.

There, of course they knew that none of us had ever gotten into anything like this before, and they were very kindly trying to walk me through each of the steps. I said that I would contact the funeral home, and that I had already spoken to Pastor Oberg who would be officiating at the funeral.

Next, they explained that they were just finishing up on a few more things in the condo, but that I would be able to come over tomorrow. They may still have to have one officer on hand while I was there, but I would have access to every area so that I could go ahead and handle whatever had to be done. I explained that my friend Lola, who had been a friend of Ella's also would be coming with me if that was OK with them, and they gave me a go ahead on that. I said that we would be over tomorrow morning, asking if about 10:00 would work, and they assured me that would be fine.

When I gave Lola that news and asked her if she would come over with me, she said that would be just fine. *You're getting closer, Bill - hang in there just a while longer and you won't have to worry about anything anymore. You'll be home free, ready to go ahead and make plans with Lola.* I soon started feeling very relaxed and gave Lola a hug and smiled down at her, adding "I love you," just to make both of us feel better. She then said, that if there wasn't anything else that she could do for me, perhaps she'd better go home, but she'd come back here tomorrow about 9:30 AM and go over to Ella's place with me. She'd make a list of what we needed to get and bring it with her. I thanked her for everything - said good bye when she was ready to leave and started feeling that I was really in control of myself and everything else. This would be a most important day - one where I had to be extremely careful - I would have been dreading it completely, but at least I knew that Lola would be with me and be watching over me. That was good, but in a way that was scary too. Hopefully I won't get caught up on anything - I had to admit to myself that I was trying to make myself look a certain way and act a certain way - *well why not - seems to me all of the time when I was having my break down that's all I did - pretend to everyone that everything was just fine, and that worked for most people, but Mom and Dad knew that something was wrong. I just have to work hard not to slip up on anything. Just so I get by with everything as far as Lola is concerned. Well, maybe I'd better take account of the fact that the police seemed to think everything was OK - yes, just concentrate on that and try to act as normal as possible.* By 9:00, I think I was doing well - ready to get through what would probably be a difficult day, but the victory will be great - just remember that. Here goes!!!!

When Lola arrived about 9:30, although my outer disposition was that of a sad person, I was beginning to thoroughly enjoy everything. In my mind I was gloating over my success. I hadn't felt happier or freer since I could even remember. I was feeling both sly and triumphant.

I was so sure of myself that I was ready to face anything. Lola sort of told me what she thought we would have to pick up at the apartment and then went into meeting with the minister, mentioning some of the things that she thought would be good to have at the funeral, and then popped up with something that I certainly hadn't thought about - she suggested that she thought it would be appropriate for me to present a eulogy. I didn't know about that, but I suppose she was right. *Well, time to get over to Ella's Condo.*

Here we go, Bill - it's show time. I had kept a good head on my emotions so far and I hoped that everything would continue that way. As we walked up to the entrance, I felt a sudden feeling of almost excitement. The policeman was waiting for us and opened the door. As I walked in, I felt myself shake - I hoped that if it was noted it would be taken as just shivering - it was cold out today after all, and Lola was in front of me, so she probably wouldn't notice. I'll just stick by her I figured, then I'll probably be OK. She walked into Ella's bedroom, and I followed, just like a little puppy dog.

She went to the closet and opened it up to look at what would be something appropriate to select to put on Ella - she finally pulled out three and asked me for my opinion. I just wanted to avoid looking at them too much, so told her that she probably was much more suited to making the right decision on that than I would be, so I would appreciate it if she just went ahead and chose one. She did and found a garment bag hanging in the closet and put the dress inside. Then she went over to the dresser and started looking for underclothes. I didn't know why - after all what would be the difference? A silly detail, but I guess women feel differently about those things. "You know, she said, "It's kind of creepy going through someone else's clothes, especially when that someone was a friend who has been murdered." "I'm certainly glad that you're here with me." What if she knew the whole story? *Remember that, Bill, she thinks you're the strong one - you'll make it through - it's finally reaching the conclusion -* I just once again assured her that she would make good decisions, and said I'd get a bag to put everything in.

That's when I walked out towards the kitchen. I guess it's true that a murderer always returns to the scene of the crime. Suddenly I was terrorized - I saw the dried blood on the floor where Ella had been – somehow, I thought someone would have cleaned it up - I got a little sickish feeling. Guess the policeman noticed and said. "Are you all right?" I replied that I just wasn't prepared for seeing everything out there. I guess I must have looked pale or something, as he suggested that perhaps I should sit down for a bit, and I did. I told him that Lola needed a bag and he asked where they were and said he would get it for me. He then took it in to Lola. I guess he must have told her that I wasn't feeling so well at the moment. When he came back, I asked him if it would be OK to have someone come in and clean up the kitchen soon, and he said that could be done any time now. *Another thing to be taken care of, and the sooner the better. I didn't want to have to come back to go through other things and be confronted with that scene again. I was still trying to erase it from my mind.*

Lola came out of the room with the bag in hand but came over and sat down in a chair by me and asked if I was OK. I nodded that I'd be fine, but maybe I did need a little fresh air. I thanked the policeman, and as Lola and I walked out the door, brought my feelings full circle. This was the last bit of Ella walking out for the final time. Our next stop was at the mortuary. We pulled up to Winstead's Funeral Home - I stated to the receptionist who I was and that we were expected. She seated us and said that she'd inform Mr. Winstead that we were here. There was always something kind of creepy about a funeral home - always looked so perfect - elegant, but comfortable furniture. Always floral arrangements, usually sitting on either marble tables or brass and glass ones. There always seemed to be piped in organ music playing softly, and an almost sickening smell of flowers. Everything to supposedly sooth people at a time of grief and suffering. Well, maybe I didn't fully fill the bill, but I was a bit of an exception.

Finally, the receptionist came back and asked us to come down the hall a bit where Mr. Tom Winstead was waiting - sitting behind an impressive looking desk with a couple of comfortable looking chairs seated on the other side of the desk where he asked us to sit down. The receptionist asked if we wanted anything to drink - coffee, water or a soda? *I was tempted to say that a Manhattan would do nicely but didn't figure anyone except me would find that amusing. See, I was still in full control.* I did say that I would appreciate a glass of water, and Lola asked for coffee - just black. While she was getting that, and after introductions had been made, Lola gave him the clothes, and he said that he appreciated it and that all would be taken care of. He expressed his condolences and then said he needed some facts about Ella and then we had to make a few simple decisions.

He asked if we had an obituary written out. Lola and I had sort of figured something out, but right now I couldn't really remember much of it. Dear, efficient Lola had written it down though, and she handed it to him for his approval. He did note that we didn't have a date of death. I came close to just giving it - thankfully Lola spoke up and explained that under the circumstances, they weren't completely certain, but that the police had suggested a possible date, so the best we could do would be to use that. Amazingly, they had come up with the right date, but just an approximate time. Yes, I guess those scenes from the TV shows were correct about how well the Forensics crews could figure out times of death. Really quite amazing.

I knew some of the dates - Ella's birth date mainly - the rest I could just punt on. I gave him her maiden name, proceeded in death by husband Mac and only daughter Rosie. Survived by former son-in-law William (Bill) Anderson, and many friends. That was about it. Tom said that he would take care of getting that into the paper, and then asked about time of funeral, etc. I explained that we were meeting with the minister, so those details weren't firmed up as yet, but that I would call them in as soon as it was set. He said that would be fine, but if there was any delay for any reason, he'd like to get it in to the paper by midafternoon, and if we hadn't made complete arrangements by then, he just would insert arrangements pending, with instructions to contact the funeral home. He then showed us a few different designs for the small booklet with all of the pertinent information in it. I figured any of them would do just fine, but I was still trying to play the role of a loving and grieving person, so I couldn't just brush off the details. I chose 2, and then asked Lola, and she preferred one of them over the other, so that was the choice.

Tom then asked about what time we wanted the reviewal. I explained that we wouldn't be having one here at the funeral home - just at the church, one hour before the service.

I think I saw a raised eyebrow at that, but so it goes - it was my decision. Only other detail to take care of then was to select the casket. I dreaded that but thank goodness I had gone through it before. I'll never forget what a shock it was when Mom died. and we all had to go through this arrangement business with Dad. I had never seen a casket room before, and it had really gotten to me. They so calmly described each of the caskets, talking about choices of metal, or dark wood or oak, etc. Then all the various colors of the linings - cream colored, pink, blue, white - all soft colors. I remember that I had kept calm during the rhetoric, but that night I had nightmares about the whole scene. I think that everyone should visit a mortuary and go through a casket room when they aren't emotionally involved in having to select one for someone you loved, just so you'd be prepared.

Here we were, decision time again. I don't know if Lola had ever had to make such a decision about this - I think she was a little overwhelmed also, but she took it all in without showing too much emotion. I wanted it to be nice, but I saw no reason to go with the highest priced one, so I chose one in a medium price range, and Lola thought that was fine. She had chosen the dress, so I asked her what color would be best for the lining. She felt that the cream color would work, so that was taken care of. Being as Tom felt that this was the only other thing that needed to be taken care of, I figured that another hurdle had been completed. As is usual, however, Tom remembered to check on one more thing - did we want him to take care of ordering any flowers, or would we be doing that ourselves. I figured it was just as easy to get everything taken care of as soon as possible and in the easiest way. I told him that I would like two large baskets, one placed on each side of the casket in the church. I was a little stymied when he asked what kind of flowers, I just told him to come up with something that would look good, but knew that Ella loved roses, so may as well go with that, and whatever color he thought would fit in with the setting. He gave me a price range, and I didn't hesitate about going on the high scale for the flowers, which pleased him - sure he made some profit on that side of the market also. Oh well, why not? Now it was on to the church.

Chapter 26

THE ACTUAL FUNERAL PLANS

Lola had called Pastor Oberg before we left for the funeral home so that he'd know approximately when we would be there, and he said the timing would work out well.

When we got there, he was ready and waiting to talk to us. He seemed like a nice enough guy. I wasn't much of a church person, I'm afraid, but I had attended church with Ella on a few special occasions - you know - the Christmas, Easter times, etc., so I had met him and talked to him at least a few times. I introduced him to Lola and explained that she had been a good friend to Ella. I think he sort of winked at me when he said he was familiar with her name as Ella had mentioned her before. He then said just to call him Pastor Bob, and suggested we sit down and chat a little. He said he had most of the pertinent information which he had pulled from church records, so we didn't have to go over much of anything of that nature. He just wanted to hear a few more things. I filled in some information about family times, the company, etc. at any rate, apparently with what we said and his own knowledge of Ella and family things that she had told him, guess he could come up with something. Then he too asked if I would like to do some sort of eulogy for her. My first reaction of course would have been no, but what with Lola mentioning it before, I figured I'd better, so I said I would, but it would be short. That seemed to satisfy both of them. He asked me about the day that I preferred. I opted for Thursday - that way the obituary would get into the Sunday paper. I always had sort of strange thoughts about that. I swore that everyone opted to die anywhere from Wednesday to Friday just so their obituaries would appear in the Sunday paper - they always seemed to have pages full of them, and everyone seemed to take time out to read all of them. At any rate, Pastor Bob once again looked at his calendar and then asked if I would prefer the morning or the afternoon. I looked at Lola as I sort of questioningly said "I think the afternoon would work out fine". We decided upon 3:00. Next, he asked if I'd like the church ladies to serve something to eat after. Gosh, I hadn't thought about all of that, so Lola sort of took over. "Perhaps we could change the time to 3:30, then we could have a light supper served - the timing may be a bit better for that." By the time the service was over, then the interment, and back to the church it would be supper time." Pastor Oberg then said - "Oh, that's another thing that I was going to ask about - where will she be buried?" Gosh, I hadn't even thought about that, but then remembered that Mac and Rosie had been buried in sort of a family plot in Lakewood Cemetery and at the time, Ella had noted that there were four spots there, so room for Rosie and me also. Well, I don't think I wanted to spend eternity within the bickering family - cremation for me.   At any rate, I told Pastor Bob that it would be in Lakewood, and he asked if I had informed the funeral home of that. I told him that I would be contacting them after we had finished talking here so that they would be aware of what all might be needed. Good, that was covered. Thank goodness for these people who are familiar with all the things that need to be taken care of and are willing to help along the way. I was getting sort of boggled by all of it.

Then we got into selecting an organist - I left that up to him. He asked if we wanted a soloist - I could have gotten along without one, but Lola thought it would be nice. Bob mentioned a tenor who would usually be available, and I said that was fine. Lola mentioned having him sing "How Great Thou Art", and that was fine also. She asked about having the gathered friends sing a couple of hymns, and Pastor said that sounded very nice, and asked what she may have in mind. She suggested "On Eagles Wings" and "Children of The Heavenly Father."

I was familiar with both of those and thought they were excellent suggestions, as did Bob. He then showed us a couple of bulletins that he thought would be nice so they could print up the order of service listing songs, etc. He only asked one thing about what readings I might want. I graciously suggested that he probably had more knowledge about what Ella would have wanted than I would, so I would leave that to his discretion, and that seemed fine to him. Now finally everything seemed to be taken care of. He did ask about a reviewal, and I once again gave him my decision. He said that sounded fine. It was then that Lola threw me for a loop when she inserted that there was one thing that Ella had mentioned to her. She wanted something done that now-a-days people just don't do - she wanted the casket to remain open during all the service and then have people walk by her one more time before they closed the casket. Even Bob was surprised at that - I could see the look on his face, but who was he to go against anyone's final wishes. I guess Pastor Bob had seen the look on my face also, as he went on to ask if that was what he should do. I replied that if Lola had heard Ella request it, I guess it would be the thing to do. He nodded his head and then handed me a card with his name and telephone number on it and said that if I had any further questions or suggestions to call him at any time. Pastor Bob then went back to one more issue. He said that he would contact the church women that there would be a funeral coming up with light supper but said it would probably be better for someone to call them with any special choices or selections. Lola spoke up and said that she would take care of that detail if he would give her the woman's name and telephone number, which he hastily looked up in the directory and wrote it down on a piece of paper for her.

I can honestly say by this time I was emotionally spent, and ready to relax a little. I mentioned to Lola that it might be nice if we stopped somewhere along the way and have a bite to eat, and she said that would be very nice. I really needed some nourishment both for body and soul. I figured I'd better get the paper and pen out again and write everything down or I was sure that I may forget some very important detail. Well, I had 2 more days to get myself pulled together.

We stopped at Marty's soup and sandwich shop. That combination sounded good to me, and when I suggested it to Lola, she said that would be fine with her. I guess I just sort of sat and stared when we first sat down, and she thought perhaps I should have a glass of wine first to sort of unwind a bit. *I think she is going to take really good care of me I thought.* I certainly agreed that it would be nice to just slowly absorb everything.

When the server came to our table, we both ordered white wine, and said we'd like to wait just a bit before ordering, but I asked if possibly they could bring some garlic toast. That always tasted so good with wine, and then we'd have some to go with our soup if we wanted it also. While we waited for the wine, I took Lola's hands, which she had folded on the table, and thanked her again for standing by me through all the decisions process. I could hardly express my gratitude, but I guess she got the message. She in turn squeezed my hands and said that she was glad that she added some support for me if I needed it right about now. Then the wine was served along with the garlic toast. I gladly took a few sips, and it was very delicious. Crisp and fresh tasting, and a bite of toast along with it was very good. I just silently enjoyed it for a few minutes. We finally put in our order - the soups were so delicious at this place that you could never go wrong. I ordered one of my favorite combinations, a Ham and Cheese sandwich with a bowl of Pea Soup - then I realized that I was very hungry. Lola ordered a Chicken Salad sandwich with Wild Rice Soup. That sounded pretty good also - I was going to have to try and learn more about her favorite foods - that would be an interesting little game. We had eaten many meals together over at Ella's, and gone out for dinner, but eating at home where you could concoct anything you wanted to would be a whole different ball of wax.

While we were waiting for the food, Lola said she needed a little more help on one thing - what should be served for the light supper after the funeral. I fell back on what I remembered having at some that I had attended - assorted lunch meats and buns, maybe baked beans - salads, chips - pickles, olives, that sort of thing, and of course some cake, or bars. Then just water or coffee. She then offered one more thing - perhaps a bowl of fresh fruits, and I liked that idea very much. "OK, she said, then I think I have a good enough idea so that I can talk a little more to the women who will be serving so that they will have plenty of time to get it all organized." "Should I tell them to plan on about 150 or 200 people?" That I hadn't thought about either, but figured a lot of the Conner's people may come, and probably some from the church, etc. "Better use 200 just to be safe - if the number is closer to 150 we'll just encourage everyone to eat lots, or we'll send home doggy bags with everyone!" She just looked at me when I said that - I don't believe she found it appropriate or particularly funny, but she let it go by anyhow. No, this isn't a time to try being a smart Alac - I quickly pulled back and apologized, said I guess the strain was getting to me. Then she smiled and said it was OK, so I seemed to get by with that one.

Soon our food arrived, and we both ate mostly in silence - perhaps we were both talked out and had lots of things on our minds. At any rate, the food tasted very good, and I was enjoying it to the utmost.

After we finished, I asked her if she needed anything else before we headed home, but she thanked me and said no. She had her car at my place, so we just returned there.

She asked if I needed her for anything else this afternoon and I said thanks, but no thanks. She told me that she would get the food arranged for so that I didn't have to worry about that anymore - as if I would have, but it was nice to know that she would cover that. I didn't even ask her if she wanted to come in - just a final thanks, I'll call you later and told her to be sure and drive carefully. I kissed her and she got into her car and drove off.

Chapter 27

A FEW MORE PERSONAL DETAILS

I still had to call the funeral home to finalize everything for them. Then I supposed I should touch base with Jim, Gary and Susie and quickly bring them up to date on what was happening. I changed my clothes - into some good old comfortable sweats - then planted myself down by the little desk area and got my phone book out.

First thing on the agenda was calling Tom Winstead, which I did, and filled him in on the final details. He then said he had everything that he needed except for a list of pall bearers. Whoa, that's one I hadn't thought of, and Pastor Bob hadn't brought it up either. I figured that I'd quickly call Jim and Gary and ask them if they would. Besides, I was going to make a call to them, so I could take care of two things at the same time. Each of them had a son who was old enough to do that duty, so when they said they would do it I asked if they would check with their sons and ask them to help also. They were both very obliging and seemed glad to be able to help me out. I then filled them in with the details and that was good. We weren't always great at just chit-chatting about things, but always liked to keep in touch, and of course hearing their voices was always just a touch of home for me. I was always grateful that all of us ended up living in the same city so we got a chance to see each other. I loved being able to watch the kids grow up and hear about all that was going on for them. When their boys were younger, I always tried to get to either some of their school events - concerts, programs, etc. Or when they were in sports, I tried to get to a couple of games for each of them during the season, and they always seemed happy to see me there and thanked me for coming. I usually remembered my camera, of course, so I had printed up some nice photos of them over the years.

I then called Tom back and gave him the names of the four people that I had come up with, but that was all I could think of, but he assured me that it was not a problem, two of the fellows from the firm would be used. He told me that he had to call Pastor Oberg and clear away a few things about the funeral anyhow, so he would give him the names of the Pall Bearers so they could have them printed in the bulletin, which I thought was great, and I told him I would appreciate that, so now that was taken care of. He did ask if we needed a limo to follow the hearse to the cemetery, but I said just a plain family car would be adequate, as there would only be Lola and myself who would be riding in it. The others would be riding with their family. If Susie came and happened to be alone, she would probably ride with one of them or we could of course have her ride with us - there would be plenty of room for her. She was the next one to call.

Calling my sister would take a little longer - she loved to just make small talk and wanted me to catch her up on anything and everything. Therefore, I went to the refrig and pulled out a can of Coke before I dialed her up. I even pulled up another chair in front of me and put my legs up on it. May as well enjoy this phone call and stretch out. It was always good to hear her voice, and I was always cheered up a little no matter what mood I may happen to be in. She always was and continues to be a neat gal. Always wondered why she didn't meet up with someone and get hitched again. Well, after I had thought about it many times, I finally asked her one time, and her reply was "What? And spoil all my fun? Then she laughed and said, "I really like my freedom, and if I should marry, I'd probably lose my alimony which is pretty good income". "Don't worry about me, Bill, I have friends, and frankly my animals are just as precious to me as any kids would be - besides they don't talk back" and then she laughed. "Seriously though, both Jim and Gary's kids have always enjoyed being with me, so any time I wanted their company either I'd call them, or they would call me, and I'd have them here for a weekend." "They always seem to have a ball, and it's fun to have them for a couple of days, but then they go back home, and I don't have to worry about them - their folks can do that."

OK - ring number four - one more and I give up "Hello, this is Susie". There's that sweet voice "Hi, kiddo, it's your brother Bill". Then I went on to fill her in on what all was going on, including the dates and times involved. She of course went on to ask every detail of everything that was going to happen, including making comments about the fact that Lola had seemed to be involved in helping with the details, and giving a little kidding about it. She just then bluntly asked when I was going to take the big step and ask Lola to marry me. Before thinking, I said "I've done that". Ouch, that was a mistake. Now the questions really started rolling out. Susie had of course met Lola and had made brief references to you. I figured she must like her fairly well, or I knew that I would have heard plenty of negative things telling me that Lola wasn't good for me. By her not sounding off against Lola, I knew Susie well enough to know that she wasn't at all against my having a relationship with her, and that was, well, sort of an approval. I'm not sure if she really knew how close I had become to Lola, but on the other hand, Susie always seemed to know more about me without my having to tell her every detail. I finally laughed and said "Hey, not right now, Sis, I'll fill you in on everything soon". I did go on to say "Truthfully, Susie, that fact just sort of slipped out - what with all that was going on right now with Ella, we opted not to tell anyone about our plans until all of this stuff with Ella had been resolved, so please don't spread the word to anyone else. No, not even Jim and Gary. Give me a month or so, then I'll let you spread the word in any way - yes, I promise, as long as you promise to keep your silence." Well, that seemed to close the subject, so after just a few more questions, I told her a little white lie - that I had to call some other people, so I'd better get rolling. "Bye now Susie, I'll talk to you later.

❧

Chapter 28

TIME TO TAKE STOCK

I finally realized just how exhausted I was. I walked back into the living room, got the fleece cover from the back of the sofa, stretched out in the recliner with my remote in hand and started flipping through the stations. I found a program that looked interesting and started watching it. It was sort of strange though, it ended up being a murder mystery, and I somehow saw myself on the screen, and it was weird. I then began to remember *when I had the break down - it was always like the TV was trying to control me - it got so that I couldn't stand to watch anything, as I'd always find some connection.*

It worried me a bit in that I was dredging up so many of those old feelings. I hadn't told Lola about my break down - after all that was ancient history - why worry about it now?

I didn't think it would happen again, would it? I'd better not take any chances though.

I was just tired, maybe that's all that it was. I looked at the clock and saw that it was about 4:00, but I thought I just may go in and lay down on the bed - it was a lot more comfortable, and maybe I'd even fall asleep.

As I laid down, I realized that for the first time ever, I couldn't even wish that Lola would have stayed with me tonight - in fact I was sort of glad that she didn't make the offer, as I wouldn't have wanted to tell her no, but I think I would have had to. I suppose I could just have turned it around and said that I thought she needed a good night's sleep, but it just stuck in my head - what was wrong with me? I guess it was just all these things that kept messing up my thoughts. I'd been having to keep everything so all in order, and I'd done well so far, but suddenly things were starting to whirl around, and I felt like I was losing control. *Can't do that, Bill, there's much too much at stake right now. Let's see, that Psychologist from way back used to say breath in through your nose and out through your mouth - slowly now. Do it a few more times, and that will help to relax you and clear your head.* I think it's working, I don't feel quite so mixed up now - a few more times, and I did fall asleep. I slept for a couple of hours. Just enough to simmer me down.

I didn't really want to get up yet - I felt so nice and warm and comfortable, but some-how I thought I'd better practice a few things in my head again so I wouldn't blow anything. Maybe tomorrow I'll call the police and ask if I can come over the day after the funeral and try to get some more information about all the things that had to be taken care of. I had remembered to ask them if they had at least turned down the furnace a little so that the bills wouldn't mount so much when it wasn't necessary. I thought it was a sensible thing to do, but they gave me a funny look when I asked. Guess they don't expect people who are supposed to be in an emotional state to think of sensible things.

I had been trying to think of her lawyer's name - *I should perhaps have it written down somewhere - maybe I should go through some of my own papers this evening. I may find some clues there. Come to think of it, that's probably the same one that Conner's used, and I think I do have that information somewhere around here.* Yah, guess I'll get out the strong box and sort through that a bit. If for no other reason, I haven't checked my own stuff over for a long time, and it probably wouldn't hurt.

When I started thinking about the condo, I did remember that I needed to call a cleaning service and have them get things cleaned up there. I'd probably better call the police again and make sure it would be OK. I don't like to think about having to prowl around and look at all that blood in the kitchen again. Yuk - it was awful, and it smelled horrible too - that's probably why I got so nauseous over there, but I'm starting to feel sort of the same way again. Better go out and find something to eat - probably just hungry. I didn't have a lot on hand, so I just made a peanut butter and jelly sandwich and poured myself a glass of milk. It really tasted good, and I knew it was good for me.

Now I was starting to feel kind of lonesome - wishing in a way that Lola was with me, but I guess I wouldn't want her to see me acting nervous or anything, so I'd just have to make it through the night alone, but not for too much longer, I hoped. While I was thinking of her though, I thought I'd just give her a call - I could say I was just checking to see if the food situation for after the funeral was in order, and then just to slip in the fact that I missed her and loved her a lot. I checked my lists after I had talked to her, and things seemed to be well in hand. I suppose I may have seemed a bit cocky about that, but I couldn't tell anyone else about how well things were going other than congratulating myself, and that I did.

When I opened the strong box, it opened up lots of memories. Strange how old papers and pictures, even old bills can become a part of your history and delving into them can be most interesting. There were papers from Conner's, my old Passport, don't know why I kept it, guess just for an interest item. There were a couple of letters from Mac which had been sent congratulating me for work well done. A couple of love letters that Rosie had sent to me when she was down in Cayman with the family. I suppose I'll have to throw those away before Lola becomes my wife, but for now I simply read them, refolded them and put them back - I hadn't wanted to go this route. *Yes Dad, I know that song "Going To Take A Sentimental Journey"* yeah, I liked that one too. *My eyes closed as I remembered him singing, then suddenly Mom was sitting next to me listening also. Everything was so nice I was just floating gently away.* Then suddenly my phone rang. Did that ever startle me. Who in the devil would be calling me this evening? I dashed in to pick it up - would you believe, another stupid recorded solicitation call.

What a dumb thing to interrupt such a peaceful scene. I tried to recapture it, but it just wasn't working.

I went back to the strong box again and pulled out a couple of things that might come in handy and put it back on the side of the closet in the bedroom. I didn't have anything else to do right now, and frankly I was afraid to watch any more TV - I knew how that had flipped me out so many years ago - best just to avoid it. I thought about going out for a short walk, but it was just too nice and warm and comfortable in here.

I paced for a while, then finally thought I may as well take a shower and crawl in bed, so that's what I did. I turned on the clock radio and had some soft background music going.

I laid there for over an hour before falling asleep - I knew that because the clock radio had gone off. I still felt kind of relaxed though, so I just pushed the button again and drifted off to lullaby land - couldn't remember just when I fell asleep, but much to my surprise and delight I did sleep - at least until about 5:30 A.M. Another big day to face.

Chapter 29

THE DAY BEFORE THE FUNERAL

I got up at that point and made a pot of coffee for myself. I turned on the TV to CNN for a while to catch up on some National news. I hadn't really been keeping up with what was going on in the world, so maybe that would be good for me. I poured myself a cup of coffee and headed for the recliner. I was pretty sure that the paper wouldn't be delivered as yet, but just had to open the door to check. Yes, I was right. It usually was here, however by 6:30, so not much longer to wait. The news reports were terrible as always. More war news, more stock markets dropping news. More gas price increases. More big executives found to be involved in using their investors monies. Why is it that they never seem to find anything nice and happy to report on anymore?

Maybe there just isn't anything like that in the news anymore. Or is it that most people only want to hear bad things? Now there's a depressing thought. One more cup of coffee before breakfast. Oh good, here's the final bit - usually about travel or nature, and the photography was so outstanding. They never said anything during these segments, only the background noises, birds chirping, the sound of the waterfalls, etc. *What I wouldn't have given to be able to make a living for myself all these years by becoming a wild life photographer.* I always had to pull myself back to reality when I started back on that old dream. I also remembered reading accounts of how they had to spend hours in a swamp, covered with mosquitoes just waiting for a glimpse of some exotic animal or see some gorgeous bird landing in a tree. Yes, nothing is perfect, that's for sure.

Finally, I heard the paper being delivered. I waited until I didn't hear him anymore and then opened up the door and pulled it inside. I flipped through and found the obituary section and opened it up to see Ella's listed. It was a fairly long one, as I had included some info about the association with Conner's company, and also about Rosie's scholarship fund, as I had placed that foremost in lieu of flowers. All of the other information seemed correct, so that was taken care of properly.

I guess I felt so smug and satisfied with that that I began to feel hungry. I wondered if I had any bacon and eggs on hand - I searched through the refrigerator and found that I had 4 eggs and about 6 pieces of bacon. Enough to fix a fantastic breakfast and still have something left over, so that's what I did. I watched it all very carefully, setting the table in between peeks at everything so that all would be ready at the same time. I poured a glass of juice and put down the toast. I remembered that I had some jelly, and that completed the picture. Except for one more special touch - *it was Dad singing "I'm Cooking Breakfast for The One I Love." I think he said someone by the name of Fanny Bryce sang it in an old movie.* I had no idea who she was, but he said she was famous many years ago. A most peculiar name, I always thought. It was a very lilting happy tune, and a fun one to hear, so it was making my breakfast even happier. The only thing that could have made it better would have been if Lola were sitting on the other side of the table. One of these days!! I savored every mouth full of food, and I have to say that it was a most wonderful breakfast - I needed to keep myself full of energy and ready to face whatever may come up. Yes, that was highly important.

After I got the kitchen cleaned up, it was about 8:30, and I figured that she would be up by now, so I dialed the phone. I heard perhaps a slightly sleepy voice answer with "Good Morning, this is Lola!" I replied, "Then I think I have the right number, is this the beautiful Lola who will, I hope before too long, become Mrs. Bill Anderson?" She laughed with that sweet little laugh that was just hers alone. "Indeed, you have the right number, now who might this be?" "Cute return", I chuckled, I missed you so much I just had to call and hear your voice". Then I asked her if she had gotten her paper in yet, but she hadn't. "Well, I just want to report that the obituary notice is in, and everything is satisfactory". She thanked me for telling her that. Then I went on," I was wondering if you were available and would like to, I'd very much like to take you out for dinner this evening". She said that would be very nice. She didn't ask where we were going, but she asked what kind of dress she should wear. I told her we'd go to a nice place, but not something real fancy, so she could use her own discretion and told her I knew she would look beautiful. Then she asked what time I would pick her up. I suggested 6:00 and asked if that would be OK, and she said that she would look forward to seeing me then, and we both hung up.

I felt on top of the world I saluted- *another song, Dad, "I'm Sitting on Top of The World". If I can only make Lola as happy as you always made Mom happy.* I found that now when I thought of Dad singing the songs, I started singing the songs too. I suppose some people thought that odd, but it was fun to do.

I took my last cup of coffee back into the living room and sipped it as I read the rest of the paper. I found it fascinating that I could feel so relaxed. *Congratulations, Bill, you're doing wonderfully - everything in place, down to the last detail.*

I knew there was one more thing to do, and that was to write a eulogy oh well, easy to write - I didn't have to verify with anyone if all I said was true, just give enough facts and figures so that it sounded good. I was suddenly looking at this as if I was doing an old school project in English. You know the kind - can't be over 600 words so it doesn't take long to read it. No extra fluff along the way. Watch the content and stick to the subject. I really used to be pretty darn good in English, so this shouldn't be too difficult. And I sat down at the computer, pulled up the word processor software and started out with a nice clean page. I set the font rather large, so I'd be able to read it more easily, and double spaced. Less likely to get lost and goof up. I never had enjoyed speaking before people, so this was not the happiest choice I would have made, but I guess it just seemed like the right thing to do. Laughingly, I thought about how many words I would put down on the paper and figured out how many thousands of dollars each word would be worth when it finally came down to settling the estate. Bet most writers would be writing frantically to think of every description they possibly could for every situation, just to watch the word count rise higher if they were being paid a goodly amount for every word. This might just be a fun project - here goes.

I started out of course by telling how I had worked at Conner's and met both Mac and Ella many years ago - rambled on about that for a while. Then went in to how I worked with Rosie and eventually we fell in love and were married so now I actually was a part of the family. I didn't really come out and talk about divorcing her. I figured that the people who knew would know, and for others who didn't know, it wasn't going to make any difference anyhow. Just talked about how suddenly she died, and how difficult it had been for Ella to first lose her husband, and within a few more years had lost her only child also.

Then I ended up by telling how blessed I was to be able to have a good relationship with Ella and that we had become good friends and ended by relating how much I would miss her, but I would always have many fond memories. There - I pulled up word count, and it was about 700 words, that was OK, and I think I got most everything down that was necessary. I pulled up spell check, made a couple of corrections, and then read it over a couple of times to see if I still approved of what I had written. I went over a couple of things, putting it a little differently in my head, but made a decision that I'd just leave it like it was. Seems to me I heard once that you're usually better off doing that, because once you started to change a few words here and there you sometimes lost the meanings and had to start all over. *Good job, Bill. It's done.* I then printed out two copies - just in case, as they say, and then I was finished.

Chapter 30

A LITTLE TIME TO RELAX

By now it was almost five o'clock. I had just lounged around today, so I thought I'd take a shower and get freshened up before I went over to pick up Rosie, *whoops, better not let that name pop up in your head again - I meant to say Lola.* Guess I had been doing a little too much looking backwards. Time to just march forward. This evening will be a good one, I'm sure of that, and then there's only one more day to have to get through, and it will be easy street. *Oh yeah, here's a song I remember, Dad and I actually started belting out "Here Comes The Sun, - Little Darlin', It's All Right Here Comes The Sun."* That's how things are going to be, Lola - happy sunshiny days ahead.

I got showered, dressed, wearing a dress shirt, but not a tie, and my sweater vest over that. That combination usually worked out nicely for casual or just sort of semi- dressy situations. I had debated quite a bit about where I should take her tonight. We had gone to several places, and we both had a few that we liked better than others. At this point I wanted to select a place that was on her "favorites" list. I then remembered that one that we had tried out a couple of months ago. It wasn't too far away, *let's see, what was the name of that place - head don't fail me now. I could see it in my mind's eye - it was an upstairs setting overlooking a lake.* Of course, we'd be looking out at ice on a pond now, but that wasn't the main feature. They had some unusual choices on their menu, and I had to admit that the food was extremely tasty. It just wasn't the style that I liked - sort of modern and simple, but they did have table cloths on the tables, and we had both agreed that the service was very nice. I loved the "Up North" look with knotty pine, logs, I suppose that was possibly just a more manly setting, and this place was more something that a lovely, refined, sweet lady would like, and that was my Lola. *Let's see now, was it Lakeview? No, keep trying- Lakeshore? Obviously, it must have something with Lake in it.* Oh yes, Crystal Lake Inn. I figured that I may as well call and make a reservation, just in case. Hated to drive any distance and then not be able to get in. Then it was a problem to have to start thinking all over again. I did call, and they made the reservation, so that was taken care of.

I got my overcoat out and put it on - yes, the one that I had worn when what I think I'll just call the last time I saw Ella - appropriate enough. I then drove over to pick up Lola.

It was just about 6:00, I figured we'd have plenty of time to get to the Inn, but I didn't want to be late and possibly lose our reservation. She looked very nice - wearing a gray skirt and, well I guess you'd call it a deep aqua sweater. I was always proud to show her off whenever we went anywhere, and this would not be an exception. I of course also told her that she looked very lovely - every woman likes to hear that. I helped her on with her coat and we were off for the evening.

When we were riding, she finally asked where we were going, so I told her that we were heading for the Crystal Lake Inn. She was very happy with that choice and seemed both surprised and very pleased that I had remembered that she liked it so much. It was dark out by the time we got there, and the place was lighted with several candles, and I did have to admit that it looked very warm and charming. There was a fireplace with a real fire going in it, and they seated us down not far from it. Just the right distance away so that we felt a little warmth from it, but not too much to get uncomfortable. We also had a window close by. Yes, as I mentioned, it was dark, but they had strings of white mini lights strung out around many of the trees outside, and it really looked like quite a fairy land. I guess my opinion of the place was rising higher than I had remembered it before.

The menu had a great variety of things. I thought the pork

tenderloin sounded wonderful, so that was my choice. Lola ordered a chicken breast stuffed with various items. Sounded a little messy to me, but as long as she enjoyed it, that's what counted. I splurged and ordered a bottle of wine - knowing that we usually seemed to agree on similar white wine choices. This was a brand that had impressed me once when it was served at someone's house a few years back, but I remembered it, and had picked it up for myself many times over the years when I was having someone over.

They actually had a wine steward who brought the bottle over, doing all of the proper opening of the bottle, pouring some for me to taste and leaving the cork. After my approval, he poured each of us a glass and then placed the wine in an ice bucket by the table. I could see that Lola was truly enjoying all of this. *Just wait Lola, I thought, I'll wine you and dine you like you've never been treated before. You'll be my Queen, my special Angel.*

They brought out a small loaf of bread sitting on a wooden carving board along with a serrated knife to cut it with. It was warm and smelled delicious. I was always happy when they brought some bread to have with the wine. That was a winning combination as far as I was concerned. This time the butter was even of spreading consistency. Sometimes you got nice fresh bread and then you made holes in it when you tried to spread some hard, cold butter on it. Yes, the index rating was going higher all of the time. After a comfortable amount of time, they brought the salads. Just mixed greens, but they were good, fresh and crisp, and the dressing was very tasty.

Then they served the main dish, and it looked most excellent, and once I got around to tasting it, I had to give that a high rating also. I asked Lola how hers was, and she sort of rolled her eyes and said it was marvelous. Who knows, this could end up being on the choicest list for both of us in the future. The waiter poured out the rest of the wine, dividing it up between us, and that worked out just right. We both ate at a leisurely pace, and didn't really talk a lot, I guess neither of us wanted to just talk about what tomorrow would bring, and just wanted to enjoy a festive, but quiet evening enjoying being with one another

- perhaps even reaching another level in our relationship - enjoying just being quiet in one another's company, not having to worry about making conversation just for the sake of conversation. It was so nice, I really didn't want it to end. When they cleared away our dishes, they asked if we'd like dessert. Lola shook her head saying she was just too full. I too had had enough to eat, but I asked her if she wouldn't at least like a cup of coffee, and she agreed to that. *Good, I thought - we can hold on to this lovely evening for just a little while longer anyhow.*

Finally, it was time to go, but this was one of those memory making evenings that I knew I would treasure for years to come, and I hoped that Lola would feel that same way about it. Obviously she did, for when we got in the car, she reached over and kissed me and said "Thank you so much, Bill, that was just about the most perfect meal I've ever had, in the loveliest restaurant, the servers were so nice, and you of course were the best looking guy around, and darn sweet to boot.", and she gave me a kiss on the cheek. How great our lives would be once we were really together.

When I got her home, I stepped inside for a bit, but figured this just wasn't the right time to make any further advances towards her, or to expect any from her either.

I just held her in my arms, giving a few passionate kisses, and then said that I'd better go before I found it any more difficult to leave. She smiled and agreed. I somehow floated on clouds as I got back into the car and drove home. It had been a perfect evening.

I thought that I'd just be able to crawl into bed and fall asleep, but even though I'd had such a nice evening with Lola, I started thinking more and more about all that would go on the next day, and I became more and more nervous. I tried all of the deep breathing exercises trying to calm myself down, but I just seemed to get more and more agitated. I turned on the clock radio but found myself straining to hear every word of every song instead of letting it calm me down. Now I was getting angry at myself - I was so near the completion of everything, I just couldn't afford to do anything wrong now. *Mommy, Daddy, what can I do - please help me find the answer. You always helped me find the answer.*

I was getting more and more upset. I finally got up and went into the bathroom and rummaged in the medicine cabinet and came up with the sleeping pills again. I debated about taking two, but I was fearful also of not wanting it to be too effective. I remembered once after I'd had the breakdown and occasionally had to use the pills because I was so depressed. I had one night taken two, and the next day was awful. Sure, I fell asleep, but the next morning was not good, - my speech was even sort of slurred. No, can't take any chances on that. Therefore, I took a pill, and made myself a cup of cocoa. That seemed to be a good combination, and within about another hour, I had fallen asleep.

Chapter 31

THE DAY OF THE FUNERAL.

I woke up about 6:00 A.M. the next morning. I didn't feel completely refreshed, but at least I had gotten some sleep, and I vowed that I was not going to do anything but think pleasant thoughts all morning. It was easy to think thoughts about Lola and that made things better. As I brewed a pot of coffee, I thought about last night. That really had been fabulous. OK, just concentrate on Lola.

I thought back on how it had been Ella who had brought us together - thank you for that Ella. Yes, I was going to concentrate on all things that were positive items. Leave out the negative *Yes Dad, I remember "You've Got to Accentuate the Positive, Eliminate the Negative, Latch on To the Affirmative, and Don't Mess with Mister In Between."* A rather strange song, but the message came through anyhow.

When I was fully awake and had some breakfast and a second cup of coffee, I got out the pen and paper and decided that I'd better actually write things down and check them off - sort of like the Christmas Song - Santa Claus is coming to town.

"Making a List - Checking It Twice". OK - I'd better call Winstead's this morning for a "last minute" check, then contact Pastor Oberg to check everything over with him. Guess that's about all I could do now. I was pretty sure that they both had gone over everything very carefully, and I would just have to trust them.

I then called Lola about 8:30 – I think I needed some assurance by hearing a familiar voice. I asked her if she wanted me to pick her up so

we could go to the church together, and she said that would be good. I
suggested that it would probably be a good idea if we got there early so
that we'd have a chance to talk to the minister again, and that it might
be a good idea to go downstairs in the kitchen to see if all was going
well for serving the meal. That would also give me an opportunity to
find out how much it would cost so that I could settle-up with them
after. I then told her that I should probably pick her up about 1:00 so
we wouldn't have to rush or, if she was so inclined, I could pick her up
about noon and we could stop at the deli restaurant and have a sandwich
before. She however thought it might be just as well to just have a quick
bite beforehand and stick to the time of 1:00, so that was arranged for.

It was only 10:00 now, so I had some time on my hands. Today
that didn't seem like such a good idea - I really would have liked some
company, as I was feeling kind of spacy, and I didn't like the feeling, it
made me nervous. I needed to hear from someone, so I opted to call
Susie. I wasn't sure if she was coming to the funeral, so figured that was
reason enough to call. That's what I started out with when she answered
the phone, and she said that she would be there. Jim had called and
asked if she wanted him to pick her up and ride with them, and she had
accepted, so that was taken care of.

Then, as I had hoped, she just started chatting a bit. I asked her
how all the animals were, and that was worth lots of conversation. I
knew of course that was always an easy in. She loved to fill the ear of
anyone who might be interested. I did find out that one of her horses
had gotten a bad gash on his side. Seemed he found some barbed wire
in a spot where he shouldn't have been in the first place, and apparently
tried to squeeze through. At any rate, it wasn't drastic, but quite deep,
so she had to be doctoring him and making sure it didn't get infected.
Think it was Chief. I really couldn't tell the difference between the
horses, so just getting to know their names was doing well enough for
me. She only had one dog now, Jazz - a mutt (I always thought they
were the best kind) who looked like a black lab, but not sure exactly
what all. She was a sweet dog though, and Susie adored her. There were
also a few cats wandering around - I know she knew each of them by

name and loved them. I was prone just to call "Here, Kitty, Kitty" when I saw one of them around. Some were inside cats, and some were barn cats, but Susie took care of all of them very well. Finally, after she had given me the run down on all of them, I figured I'd better hang up and start to get myself ready. I relayed that to her, adding that I would be seeing her soon anyhow, and the conversation was ended.

By then it really was time to get dressed. Lola had helped me make the decision as to what I should wear last time she was over, so I had everything in mind. We both decided on my best navy-blue suit. Then I had a deep maroon shirt, and a tie that was predominately dark blue, but with some of the same color maroon in a small design. It did look quite dignified and nice, so I felt confident that we had made a good choice. After I got dressed, I made sure that I had my credit cards, my check book and a copy of The Eulogy. Oh yes, mustn't forget a handkerchief. One never knows, even if I didn't really get emotional about everything, it wouldn't hurt to take out a hanky and sort of pretend that I was a little emotional. *Good thinking, Bill.* Finally, it was time to go. I put on my overcoat, shut the door behind me and left to pick up Lola. *This is it, Bill - SHOW TIME!!!*

When I got to her place she was, as usual just about set to go - only had to check on a couple of more things, and within five minutes, we were in the car and on the way to the church. I didn't really talk too much, and neither did she - I guess I was afraid that I might slip up somehow, and I suppose she probably was really having issues over memories of Ella, also just respecting my space. We had become much more careful about each other's feelings and seemed to know when to talk and when to stop. There weren't many cars in the parking lot at the church yet, so we got a prime spot. The hearse was there already, so I assumed that all was on schedule with Winstead's. She and I walked in - boy you sure could smell flowers - Even though the obit had said to give to the scholarship fund in honor of Rosie, for the heart fund or for a donation for the person's favorite charity, there seemed to be a myriad of flowers that were being brought in. I really wasn't interested in looking inside the church right now. Just checked the Narthex to see that things were in place there. Tom already had a small table set out with the small folders with all the factual information about Ella in it, the bulletins, a guest book to sign, and an attractive large box with a slot in the top for cards to be dropped into. He asked me if I would care to walk down and view Ella first before anyone came. I didn't want to, but I couldn't very well just say that, so I explained that we were going downstairs to talk to the women there and Pastor Bob wanted to talk to me for a moment. Well, that could have been a slight exaggeration, but I did want to make sure that I'd be able to give the checks for the organist and the vocalist to him so that he could pass them on. I had remembered envelopes, but I honestly wasn't sure of their names, so I'd need to find that out so that I could make out checks.

First though, Lola and I walked downstairs. Everything looked very nice - not just like a basement of a church. I had never been down there before, and it really was very pleasant looking. They had a variety of tables, some round, some long to seat about ten people and some smaller ones that seated about six. They all had color coordinated plastic tablecloths on them, and small bouquets of flowers. The serving tables were all set up already. Things like buns, butter, assortments of lunch meats, salads, bars, cakes, etc. already on the table covered with plastic wrap. There was a very nice large bouquet in the center. I thought the flowers were real, but Lola assured me that they were just nice quality silk ones, but she too thought they were very attractive. The plates were on a cart at the end of the tables, ready to pick up and fill as you went along and helped yourself with whatever food you may want to have. When we got down there, the women were setting up the tables with napkins, silverware, cups and glasses. They apparently were going to have carafes of coffee and water on each table, and I thought that was very nice. I then asked who was in charge and they pointed me in the direction of Mrs. Bloomberg. She was very pleasant looking, with a big smile for us when we introduced ourselves. I asked her how much we owed her. She said she thought it would be about four hundred and fifty, saying that of course the bars and cakes were donated. At any rate, I said I would take care of it.

Then it was time to go up to meet with Pastor Oberg. We walked down the hall from the sanctuary to his office. The door was open, and he asked us both to please come in. He closed the door after us so that we'd have a little more privacy. He asked first if there was anything else that we wanted done which hadn't been covered yet, but I told him that I felt everything had been handled nicely. I did tell him that I would like to get the checks made out for the organist and the soloists if he would please give me their names and the suggested honorarium to give to them. I suppose this is always a little bit of a touchy situation, but I took out my check book. He told me each of their names and said usually it was One hundred fifty dollars for the organist and one hundred for the soloist. I took it from there and made one out for one hundred fifty for the soloist and two hundred fifty for the organist. I then asked if he would see to it that they received the envelopes, and he said he'd be happy to do that. I then asked about the check for the lunch, if it should be made out to the church or to Mrs. Bloomberg. He suggested that I might just make it to Mrs. Bloomberg, but make a notation on the check to WELCA, which was the women's church organization. I made that one out for seven hundred and fifty dollars. After all, I knew that Ella had been involved with that and she would want it to be done right. I also had one for him, of course that I had prepared at home, so I handed that one to him at the same time. He thanked me for all of them. Then he suggested that perhaps we should have a time to pray together. I wasn't much for this kind of thing, but Lola immediately closed her eyes and folded her hands in her lap, and I followed and did the same.

I then asked what the usual procedure was, and he said that it would probably be just fine if I were to stand out in the Narthex of the church and greet people. He had previously showed Lola and I that there was a chapel area down by the side of the altar where we could sit if we wished, so that we wouldn't have to be in the front row to be viewed by everyone. That had indeed pleased me at the time - especially when Lola had popped up with the news that Ella wanted an open casket - at least I wouldn't have to be sitting there looking at her all the time.

I then saw that Jim and Mary, Gary, Sally and their kids and Susie had all arrived. I asked them if they had been instructed by Tom as to what procedures would be followed, and they assured me that everything was under control. They too would be sitting in the chapel area, and that really made me feel better - I hadn't been sure if they had to sit in the front pews or not. Now I knew that I would have a good support group, and everything would be OK.

Soon it was time to take our appointed spot, of course I had asked Lola if she minded standing there, and she agreed. My brothers and sisters milled around also, so that helped too.

By this time, a lot of people were arriving. I guess I was surprised to see how many friends Ella had, or maybe they were all just friends from Mac's business connections. I suppose that some of them could be people that she had known from working in the consignment shop. I did see some familiar faces that I knew from Conner's, and they came over to shake hands. Most of the board of directors were there, and of course I knew them and at least could make some small talk. There was only one that annoyed me - he had to ask if the police had found out anything new. I didn't really think this was the time or place to bring the whole thing up, but I tried to cover up quickly. I just said "No, nothing that they have informed me of anyhow." I then changed the subject as quickly as possible. As it got more and more crowded, it became noisier and noisier, and I was beginning to feel very agitated. As they walked over to talk to me, I found that I was only vaguely listening to them as they extolled about what a fine woman Ella was and all the great things that she had done.

The voices just became a faint, rambling chatter. *I certainly could have told them what a fine woman she was - that picking, picking, picking. The blue tie didn't go with the brown suit - stand up straight - don't mumble when you speak - eat everything on your plate - don't eat your pie with a spoon - don't sniff, use a handkerchief.* Everything was going wild in my head. *Suddenly I wondered if it would have pleased her to know that I had a white handkerchief in my pocket the night that I killed her. That was quite amusing, I thought. I think I started to sort of snicker, but I guess others thought I might have been chocking back some tears.* Better cover that, Bill - *I pulled that lovely white handkerchief out of my pocket and just sort of passed it over my nose.* Good show, Bill. Lola gave my arm a quick, hard squeeze. *Me crying over Ella! That was even funnier than the last thought, but I couldn't lose control of myself. Everything had gone all right so far, and I wasn't going to spoil anything now.* Most of the people were starting to go into the sanctuary now, and the organist had started playing. Jim had been watching me quite closely and walked over and asked if I was OK. I nodded, but he suggested that I'd maybe better get a drink of water before we went in to sit down. I said that would probably be a good idea.

As we went by the water fountain, I did get a drink, and that sort of cleared my head somewhat. Then Tom said it was time for us to go in, so he would escort us down to the side entrance so that we wouldn't have to walk down the middle aisle. Saved again. Finally we were seated, *now however, another thought came into my mind - just think, as Pastor Oberg started with "We are gathered together to honor the memory of Ella Conner" I had a weird thought. right here all together was the murdered woman, and the man who had murdered her who was pretending to be mourning for her. What a picture.*

The soloist sang then and brought me back to my senses. *Maybe it was time for a few deep breathing exercises, only just do it gently, not with too much gusto or everyone might notice.* Pastor Oberg then stood up and read the "fact sheet" as I so fondly had referred to them on such occasions. You know, Date of Birth, Date of Death. When she and Mac had been married, all that sort of thing. Then the people sang "Children of The Heavenly Father". I remembered that song with some fondness. Ironic that Lola had suggested that one. We had chosen that song to be sung at both Mom and Dad's funeral. Mom especially had always loved that hymn so much and knew most of it by heart. I even joined in on singing that one. There, that's better. Somehow at the right time, I manage to walk up to the lectern area and read the Eulogy. I think I did OK. All I know is that I managed to find a route behind the flowers so that I didn't have to go by the coffin and look at her.

Everything was really working out very well. The minister said a few more words, then the people sang "On Eagle's Wings". I didn't really sing, I became fascinated watching all of them, and saw that many of them were really crying. Somehow, I never realized that there were lots of people there who must have really been Ella's friends. I don't know why this hit me as strange, after all, Lola had been her friend, or no, not really, she had been Rosie's friend, but then became Ella's friend. *I was beginning to feel more and more mixed up and strange thoughts were entering my head. I remembered when I had the break down, Mom and Dad were always careful not to say that I was thinking strange things, it was just that my mind was playing tricks on me, and I had become convinced that they were right. After all, Mom and Dad were always right - weren't they?* OK Bill, get back to what is going on. The minister then said a few more things, the soloist sang a final song, and finally it was all over. Then I knew it was time that we had to walk by the coffin to pay our last respects. *Suddenly my mind rambled and I wondered how they had been able to fix Ella up - how they could cover the knife wound so it wouldn't show -* I was getting scared. Pastor Bob gave us a nod - that meant that we should come up, and I was kind of frozen. Finally, Lola sort of pulled my arm gently, and somehow, I started walking. Then we were in front of Ella and I stared down at her. *They hadn't fixed her up at all. I looked at Lola - she was looking at me very strangely - how could she not see. It was still there - the blood was still on her blouse. The knife was still in her throat and the blood was still oozing out over the cream colored gathering in the coffin lining. Her eyes were staring at me, filled with horror, and I then heard her whisper "Why?"* I felt my hands go to my head and I started screaming. I heard myself say "She's still like she was when I killed her" I repeated it over and over. I tried to stop. I knew everyone was looking at me with that same horror in their eyes as Ella had, but I couldn't stop. Then I fell to the floor.

I don't remember much after that. I don't know exactly what happened. Everything's very quiet right now. All that I hear are the two men dressed in white talking to one another at the foot of my bed.

I do hear one more thing though. I keep asking the other people here in this strange place, but they say that they can't hear it. I know though that they must, as the noise echoes from one wall to the other. It alternates, first softly, then really loud. Don't you hear it? It's echoing softly now, but listen closely, you'll hear it. There, that time it was really loud - you must have heard it that time. That was Ella, sounding the gurgle of death.

THE END

www.ingramcontent.com/pod-product-compliance
Lightning Source LLC
Chambersburg PA
CBHW071829190726
48292CB00005B/1691